WRITHE

ERICA SUMMERS
+
H. M. WOHL

WRITHE

WRITHE
By Erica Summers & H. M. Wohl
Copyright © 2024 by Erica Summers
Copyright © 2024 by H. M. Wohl

Rusty Ogre Publishing
www.rustyogrepublishing.com

West Haven, Connecticut, USA

All Rights Reserved.

This book is a work of fiction. Names, characters, places, events, organizations and incidents are either part of the author's imagination or are used fictitiously.

Any resemblance to actual persons, living or dead, or actual events is purely coincidental.

Cover Art by Steve Thompson

ISBN: 9781962854269

For Rick and Dave...

*The men who encourage all of our raunchy,
disgusting conversations, ideas, and shenanigans
with a smile.*

More by Erica Summers
Vanity Kills
Bad God's Tower
The Rictus Grin & Other Tales of Insanity
Price Slashers (w/Chisto Healy and Mick Collins)
*Ensuring Your Place in Hell II (w/Stephen Cooper and
Otis Bateman)*

More by H.M. Wohl
*From Ashes: Book One of the Illuminator Saga (as
Heather Wohl)*
*Desdemona in Embers: Book Two of the Illuminator
Saga (as Heather Wohl)*

TRIGGER WARNING:

Writhe is a work of extreme horror fiction.

This novella contains heavy profanity as well
as extreme violence, gratuitous gore, and slurs
that be offensive to some readers.

You have been warned...

CHAPTER 1

December 29th

12:47 p.m.

WHAP!

Garrett Reubens knew the sound all too well. The abrupt crack of metal in the minuscule cubby that constituted a kitchen. For two grand a month, he didn't expect a stellar view of the city with lights that glittered against the Manhattan skyline like a junebug orgy. Hell, he didn't even expect a swanky elevator. He told himself the daily walks up and down would help him stay in shape. He could use what he saved in a gym membership toward his diet of shrimp Ramen noodles and employee-discounted food at the restaurant where he waited tables four days a week.

However, he *had* expected some of the bare *essentials*.

Like, a non-leaking refrigerator that had the clearance to open without smashing the cupboards in front of it. Or a toilet that didn't shake when you sat on it and properly gobbled up bowel movements like a greedy little porcelain pig.

He expected a stairwell. One big enough that he could get a decent-sized bed up instead of the box-store futon he had to order and assemble after schlepping it up two winding flights of stairs.

Most of all, he'd expected to be the only living resident there. But he wasn't. He was one of *many* beings living in the studio apartment, with its breathtaking view of a red brick wall. The neighboring high-rise eclipsed the sun and made the place feel perpetually dank.

At least he was the only *human.*

The sound of the snap made him drop the tiny wheel-and-axle assembly in his fingers to the cardboard protecting the table below. The sound scared him so much that he nearly glued his own fingertips instead of the toy Ford Fairlane model he'd been gifted for Christmas, a gift from his folks down in Jersey.

The rat died instantly. It lay motionless between the spring-loaded metal wire and balsa slab, black eyes bulging from its narrow face.

It was huge. They *all* were. It must've been the size of a goddamned rubber chicken stuffed with meat.

He grabbed his oven mitt and timidly pinched the tip of its tail, testing it with a scared jerk once or twice before picking it up. He had to ensure it wasn't playing opossum, like the last one. When that one had started squirming, he shrieked like his five-year-old niece. This time, he wouldn't make the same mistake.

He whipped the thing, intending to humanely break its neck if still alive, and then held it still. The animal hung straight down like a wet dishrag. He walked it to the window, held it outside, and looked around for people walking the sidewalk. Once satisfied that no one was nearby, he pried the bar back, and the rodent dropped like a reverse rocket. It dove to the sidewalk, landing on the snow-lined concrete with an explosive, little smack. It detonated like a tiny blood grenade, spattering a small patch of crimson onto the frozen pavement below.

Sure, he *could* have thrown it away, but then he'd have had to smell the damn thing all night. The chute at the end of the hall by Ligerski's apartment leading down into the dumpster had been plugged for months. Even with the recent Nor'easter blasting in snow and blustery air, turning Manhattan into a refrigerator, the smell near the chute was enough to make a man gag.

Garrett washed his hands in the ridiculous excuse for a kitchen sink, re-set the trap, and waltzed back to the tiny table. He cracked his knuckles and slunk into his rickety chair with a smile. "Let's see, drive train–"

WHAM-WHAM-WHAA-WHAM-WHAM.

Silence.

TAP-TAP.

Garrett rolled his eyes. He knew what the melodical and specific knock at the door meant. It was Hunter Favereau, the owner of the building, no doubt wanting another favor in exchange for some money knocked-off the rent.

Anyone else would have used the buzzer.

Whatever it was, Garrett knew he would begrudgingly do it. Manhattan had become far too expensive to turn down paying opportunities. He just hoped that whatever the favor was, it didn't involve Hunter's eleven-year-old, Hamilton. He'd rather stand on rickety scaffolding and scrub pigeon shit off every window of the four-story apartment building with his favorite wool sweater than deal with that little fuck-face.

Something in him sensed the polite yet aggravating knock would sound again, so he unlatched the chain lock, twisted the deadbolt, and opened it with a plastered-on smile. He touched the wooden baseball bat he kept beside the door with his fingertips. It was a subtle comfort to him, knowing that it was right there in arm's reach if he needed it.

As if right on schedule, there was Hunter Favereau, his fist balled at eye level, looking like he was about to do his silly little knock again on Garrett's face.

"Oh, wow, you scared me. I wasn't expecting you to answer so quickly." Hunter un-balled his hand and swiped his fingers through his dark head of hair.

"Yeah, I'm off til the second for the holiday." Garrett regretted it as soon as he uttered it. He left himself no room to lie his way out. He readjusted his body, leaning on the frame. "So, what can I do ya for?"

"I know it's last minute, but could you come over for a bit and hold down the fort with Hamilton while I run into work? A bunch of us nematologists from the laboratory are prepping for a symposium in Brooklyn on the fifth, and one of the molecular cell biologists coming in from Sweden just had a catastrophic loss at his institute. I gotta come in and find a replacement for him. He was going to be one of our keynote speakers."

"They have nematology symposiums?" Garrett cocked an eyebrow.

"Oh yeah, definitely. There've been some interesting new developments lately. See, these two men in Antarctica discovered a polychaete from the Pleistocene era that has been just *sitting,* encased in permafrost for 49,000 years in a cryogenic suspended animation of sorts. This blows that fucking 46,000-year-old roundworm discovery five years ago out of the *water*." Hunter crossed his arms, pleased, and added, "Metaphorically speaking, of course. It was in ice, not water."

"Of course." Garrett agreed as if he had any idea what the attractive geek in front of him was talking about.

Hunter continued. His oblivious, crystal-blue eyes were alight with fascination as he spoke, "They thawed these things out, and they began to spawn, reproducing at a massive rate. It's all pretty fascinating, actually."

"Sure," Garrett lied.

"I've got one at our place that I'm doing a reproductive study on right now for the symposium. We believe one of them is about to lay eggs. And, these polychaetes lay exponentially more eggs than any other worm on record, to date."

Garrett wanted to be anywhere but in the doorway leading to a drafty landing, talking to a nerd about worms. His mind drifted further away, imagining what it would be like to have enough money to take a cruise somewhere. Anywhere…

Jamaica looks nice…

"Anyway, I can see I'm boring you. I do this all the time. I get so excited about my work that I forget how dull it is to people outside my profession. A thousand apologies, Garrett. Thank you for watching Hamilton. I should only be gone for about 2 hours. You know I can't leave him alone that long. He'll burn the whole building down."

Garrett knew that there was truth in what he said. Hamilton couldn't be trusted with making a *sandwich*, much less running wild for a few hours unsupervised.

"Two hours, and I'll take $200 off the rent this month."

Garrett thought to himself for a moment. He was terribly conflicted. On the one hand, for $100 an hour, he'd consider giving some random older regular at the restaurant a hand job in the alley. *Money was money.* But on the other hand, Hamilton was akin to a fucking *demon.* He knew if you shaved the boy's hair off, there'd be triple sixes scarred into his scalp. The child was *beyond* needing guidance. A straight jacket was what the little, fat fuck *really* needed.

The urgency in Hunter Favereau's eyes alluded to his sincere desperation. His brows furrowed as he stared at Garrett, face pleading. "It's only for a couple of hours."

After a deep sigh, Garrett nodded almost imperceptibly.

Hunter thrust himself upon his renter, embracing him tightly. "Oh, thank you so much! None of the babysitters on any of the apps would agree to come anymore. Seems he's terrorized too many. We're starting to get a reputation."

"You should think about a boarding school."

"*Right*?!" Hunter chuckled, blowing the comment off, not realizing Garrett was completely serious. He realized the stressed, single dad had no plans to change anything. He was simply waiting out the clock until Hamilton was old enough to be someone else's problem.

"We'll have a fine time, I'm sure of it." As the words came out of his mouth, Garrett felt like he'd sold his soul for a couple hundred bucks. Every time he went over there to watch that little bastard, he regretted it more. Though he was only eleven, the asshole's evil powers were growing.

"You're a stellar human being, Garrett. Thank you." Hunter pointed a finger at him and drifted toward his chipped apartment door. "I'm gonna head out around, like, two."

As he heard the door shut behind the man, the faux-smile fell from Garrett's face.

CHAPTER 2

December 29th
1:34 p.m.

Luca walked along silent rows of rusty, dented lockers and read the numbers until he found his. The paint was slathered over the rust in a vain attempt to seem more presentable than they were. Luca said a silent prayer that this precinct wouldn't be like his old one, held together with bubblegum and duct tape, run by people who were counting the hours to get home. He was in this to do some good, and New York was a place where he could do just that.

He cranked the dial of the combination lock and spun it to the numbers crudely scribbled on a scrap of paper. The introduction with his new Captain had been brief and to-the-point. Today would be the day Luca's *fresh meat* dropped into the mix, distracting the men and chumming up the waters of the Midtown North Precinct.

"Luca Han, right?" A voice called out from behind him. The tone seemed friendly, but Han remained apprehensive.

These were carnivorous fish, and he was no longer in his small, comfortable pond.

"Y-yes." Luca spun to the last number from the paper and tugged upward on the locker's handle. As he pulled it open, he was greeted with a slowly expanding wall of shaving cream that filled the space within, bulging outward at him like pudge spilling from an over-cinched belt.

Han turned toward the sound of men cackling.

"Shit never gets old." One of the men in uniform reached out his mocha-skinned hand and gave a stunning, white smile. "What's up? I'm Officer Aguilar. This is Officer Fisher." He pointed his finger to the man beside him whose thinning brown hair clung desperately over the ever-widening expanse of pale, bare scalp. His thick, sausage-like fingers jutted toward Han.

"You got a baby face, Guppy."

It was something Luca had heard all too often.

Fisher chuckled. "We can use you on *Project Safe Childhood*. That there is a face the *pedo's* would love."

Luca forced a smile. "Not sure what to say to that."

Fisher scrunched his thick, brown brows. "What? It's a *compliment*."

A blonde woman's tall, slender figure in full-uniform strode into view. Her stunning features were accentuated with light makeup, and her hair was done-up in a tight bun. Her biceps more pronounced than Luca's. He felt both intimidated and turned on. Her uniform failed to hide her incredible curves. Her caramel eyes glanced at him, lingering for a moment too long. He felt his dick jolt in his pants, alive with an electric sexual current.

"The old shaving cream shit again? Fisher! You should use some of that to shave off that fucking pubic hair you've been calling a beard."

Aguilar cackled and clapped.

Fisher self-consciously stroked his goatee. "Tredo, Why the hell are you in here? And yesterday, *you* said my goatee was *growing in nicely*."

"That's a lie, Fisher. An *obvious* lie. Do us all a favor and stay out of the interrogation room. Clearly, the truth is a foreign concept to you."

Aguilar groaned with laughter and then spoke into his cupped hands like an intercom voice. "Officer Fisher, report to the burn unit…"

"Han," Tredo barked at Luca. "My partner's got the flu, so *I'm* your partner today. Let's debrief and get on the road."

Luca nodded and followed the order. The yellow hue of his cheeks flushed with excitement. He grabbed his small duffel bag and looked back at his locker. The shaving cream expanded even further, dribbling out like rabies foam from a dog's gaping maw. He doubted he could get the locker closed again without making an even bigger mess. "So, uh, where do I put my stuff? I can't just leave it here?"

"Leave it, Guppy," Fisher added bitterly. "Nobody is gonna steal it. It's a fucking police station."

CHAPTER 3

December 29th

1:59 p.m.

It was only for a couple of hours. That's what Garrett kept telling himself over and over in his head as he turned the knob on Hunter's door. He pinched his eyes tight and took a deep breath. He'd need every ounce of his cool to deal with the little prick.

Once inside, he looked around. Hamilton was sitting on the couch, engrossed in the local news, shoveling a bowl of cereal into his pudgy face. He nodded to Garrett, and he politely offered a half-wave to the little runt. He set his paperback down on the arm of the couch and headed into the kitchen for a beer.

While his ability to child-rear sucked, Hunter's taste in IPAs had always been pretty impeccable. Garrett pressed the cap against the counter and slapped it with his palm. The lid rattled around on the marble countertop and he made no attempt to throw it away.

Hunter's apartment was so much larger and more updated than Garrett's, astonishingly so. He felt a pang of jealousy as he eyed

Hunter's brand-new cappuccino maker. He wondered what it was like to live on a nematology professor's salary.

It must be nice.

"'Sup, homo? Dad making you watch me again?"

"Yeah, you're stuck with me for a couple of hours." Garrett didn't make eye contact. "And stop calling people homo, you doink."

"Why? You gonna *cancel* me?" The kid cocked a brow at his babysitter, instigating something. "You *are* a fag, right?"

"*That* word is like, way *more* offensive."

"Your lack of a *sex life* is offensive. You never have any of your little butt-buddies over." His eyes zeroed in on Garrett for a moment and then returned to the TV. "You and I share a *wall*, fuck-stick. I *know* you're not getting any ass. Or if you *are*, you're sure as hell not satisfying anyone."

"Sometimes, I swear you talk like a 40-year-old man."

"It takes one to know one."

"Kid, I'm *thirty-eight.*"

"And graying like you're fuckin' sixty. Dad says you collect baseballs and model cars and dumb shit that old *fogeys* like. You get a discount on those with your *AARP* card?"

"At least I'm not named after a Broadway show," he fired back quickly, upset that he was lowering himself to the kid's level.

"Eleven-time Tony-winner. But you already *knew* that. Probably been to it ten times, showboating for your *boyfriends*, queer."

Garrett noticed Hunter had his nematology work sprawled out on his breakfast table, a piece of furniture that was damn near the size of his whole rat-infested kitchen. On it were documents and blown-up photographs showing the icy encapsulation, thawing, and eventual life cycle of a worm. One appeared to have a tiny set of piranha-like teeth at one end of it's colorful body. It was long and segmented, magenta near the rear half and a lighter, more vibrant shade of pink near what Garrett imagined was the head. The face, *if you could call it that*, was open. The flesh was twisted back, housing several off-white toothy protrusions.

Garrett grimaced.

It looked like an uncircumcised cock with fangs.

He held up the picture, studying the grotesque enigma.

"It's one of dad's new fuckin' bugs," Hamilton said, eyes flitting across the alarmist headlines on the screen. "The real one's in his room. That's just a picture, so try not to put it in your mouth. I know it looks like what you're into suckin' on."

Garrett whipped his head around and stepped into the archway dividing the rooms. "Enough dude, Jesus Christ. What if I *was* gay? Would that make literally *any* difference in our, like, dynamic?"

"I *knew* it." Hamilton shook his head, eyes locked on the news. "Also, don't say our dynamic like I'm your fuckin' boy-toy. If I were gay, I'd pull ass a lot better looking than you."

"Oh my GOD, kid." Garrett pounded his fist into the wall. "Seriously, dude, shut up. Go back to watching *Breitbart* or *Newsmaxx* or whatever far-right bullshit you've got on, you little future-felon."

Hamilton sighed deeply. "It's *Fox*. A lot of people watch Fox."

"Yeah, future *Proud Boys* and *Q-Anon* supporters. What? You doin' a school report on *PizzaGate?*"

"You know, *you're* what's wrong with this country."

That made Garrett laugh. "Sure, kid. Next thing you know, you'll be schooling me on why *forty-five* was the literal second coming and saying things like, 'he's not a politician, Garrett. He's the messiah. He says what we're all thinking.' Dude, every time I come over to watch you, you sound more like my father."

"Shit, I'll bet your dad sounds more like this." Hamilton lowered his voice to an obviously mocking tone, pretending to be Garrett's dad, "Uh, hi. My son is a pole-smoker, and I'm never gonna have any grand kids, so I might as well blow my brains out now." He mockingly loaded an imaginary handgun and blew his brains out, spitting hunks of cereal out of his mouth in a fibrous, sugar-laden explosion.

"Yeah, nailed it, kid. That's exactly what my dad sounded like before he died." He looked at family photos stuck to the brushed metal fridge by science-themed magnets. "I mean, before that tired trucker fell asleep and smashed him into a human latke against a guardrail outside'a Stamford a few years ago, I'm *positive* my sexuality was his greatest concern."

That perked the kid up. "Seriously?" Milk dribbled down his round face as he glanced over at Garrett.

"Mmm-hmmm. Heard it shot his guts out his asshole like *that*." He snapped his fingers, still examining the contents of the room. "So yeah, bully for you, you chubby, little turd. Must be *cool* to still have a dad that's alive."

That shut the kid up for a moment. "Why you gotta fat shame me? Aren't you little Dem' snowflakes against that kinda hate-speech?"

Garrett completely ignored him, still ruffled by the crack at his dad. "Wanna talk about my *mom,* too? She had a stroke a few years back, and she's bed-ridden now in some overpriced facility down in Gainesville. Wanna do an impression of her? I can't wait to see you drool down half of your face and struggle to pick up a cup. That's gonna be a real treat for me."

Unable to fire off a retort, Hamilton slammed his bowl of milk onto the table haphazardly, sloshing the contents of it across the veneer.

Garrett closed his eyes, knowing he'd have to wipe it up. Hamilton never cleaned anything.

"Dude, you're fuckin' bummin' me out. If you talk about shit like that on your dates, it's no wonder you're keeping Jergens and Kleenex in business." He stood, clicked off the TV, and tossed the remote onto the floor.

Garrett checked his watch. "Don't children like you have nap time right about now? Maybe that's why you're cranky. Why don't you run along." He waved the kid away, taking the dripping bowl of milk to the sink. "Let me know if you need me to read you a story or anything."

Hamilton flipped him off and shuffled down the squat hallway, turning into one of the rooms without another word.

Garrett didn't know that the room wasn't Hamilton's and thought nothing of it beyond a swelling sense of relief that the pest was gone. He checked his watch, counting down the moments before Hunter said he would be home for the afternoon. That time couldn't come fast enough.

Garrett grabbed the remote, clicked through a few stations, and tried to forget where he was. He laid down, sprawling himself across the slate-gray couch and then kicking his feet up onto the arm. His eyes narrowed, and moments later, he drifted off to sleep.

***

It was less than twenty minutes later when Garrett realized he'd made a massive error in displaying any vulnerability around the little heathen.

He awoke in a panic, feeling pain sting inside of his ear. He slapped the side of his head, connecting instantly with a human hand. He could hear the devious giggle of a pre-teen above him. His heart pounded, and he sat up in a flash, feeling something wriggle in his ear despite Hamilton being several feet away now. He reached up to feel what it was, and his finger connected with something worm-like.

Garrett grabbed hard and tugged, pinching the writhing thing. He yanked hard despite the acute pain. It felt like a sharpened pencil was being stabbed into the canal. He felt the thing curl and grip, its texture more like suede than a water-balloon.

It was climbing inside.

Seeking shelter.

Gnawing.

Tunneling.

Garrett screamed, pulling hard again. He could hear Hamilton's voice in his other ear. The roar and cackle of the kid's hearty laugh made his blood boil. The little fuck looked like an overjoyed baby, the only fat infant with nefarious intentions. He wanted to slap the little shit right across his giggling face.

Garrett groaned, feeling the strong little thing slither deeper. He pinched it and pulled hard, holding it as if it were an undulating Q-tip. Suddenly, he could've sworn he felt the soft, fleshy thing tear into two, but the body of it came free with a grotesque tearing sound, magnified like an amplifier in his head. He pulled away the hunk squeezed in his fingertips and studied at it, heart thudding.

All those tiny legs.

The spinules…

The violet stripe that undulated up the center of it was like the shit-filled vein on a shrimp through its bright pink body. Dark brown gunk oozed out of its midsection, like mud, onto his fingers.

And where was its head?

He couldn't tell if he had his fingers on that end or not. It wriggled in his hand so fast that he couldn't tell if it was intact or severed.

He slung it at the floor and watched its kinked, segmented body riot as if skewered by a hook and dropped into a lake for fishing bait.

Despite the disorientation from being awakened in such a violent manner, he recognized it immediately from the photo, it was the thing in the photos on Hunter's table. It was the thing with four, tiny, needle-like teeth. He rubbed his ear, unable to tell if the pain was phantom and simply lingering in his mind or if there really was still a piece of the thing jammed inside of him.

He could picture the coppery fangs in the photo still trying desperately to penetrate the walls of his cochlea.

Despite it being a harmless prank, he felt assaulted. He stood, and a wave of nausea and adrenaline washed over him. He wavered, discombobulated. Feeling *sick.*

Terror coursed through him, soon replaced by fury. The sound of the kid's cackling weaved in and out as his mind struggled to piece together what happened.

Garrett emitted a furious roar and snatched the child up by the collar of his milk-stained tee.

The muffled voice of the crotchety neighbor on the other end of their floor wafted through the thin walls. Ms. Ligerski was complaining again, as she often did about the noise in the building. She yelled something unintelligible. He paid no attention to the protests of the old bag, instead focusing on the drilling pain that throbbed inside his head and his intense desire to pummel the juvenile in his grasp.

"What the *hell*, kid?!" Garrett's panicked voice echoed off the walls. "Are you freaking *kidding* me?"

"Dude," Hamilton laughed like an evil chipmunk, and Garrett released his grasp, whipping the kid backward. Hamilton was unfazed by it and doubled over, clutching his aching belly rolls as he juddered with laughter. "You… are *such*… a pussy!"

Garrett rubbed his aching ear, eyes drifting to the floor where the thing still squirmed. It was no longer oozing. Its ends both looked pink and fleshy from afar as it twirled in its own slime and muddied secretions.

"You know what?" Garrett balled his fists. "I don't need this crap."

As he stormed across the room and whipped open Hunter's front door, he saw Ms. Ligerski with her wrinkled face hanging out of her open apartment door at the end of the U-shaped floor near the stairs ascending to the fifth floor.

"*What?!*" The question came out like the bark of a dog. One trying to be threatening… and *failing*.

"Keep it down, peckerhead! Jesus Christ, if it ain't the bastard upstairs tap dancing like he's auditionin' for a fuckin' musical, it's you over here screamin' like a goddamned *girl*."

"Oh, shut *up*." He sneered. His brown eyes squinted, face scrunched in disgust. "Mind your business." He offered, drifting back to his doorway and slipping inside.

As the door slammed, Ms. Ligerski hollered out in a nasty tone, "I *would*, but you are being so loud you're *making* it my business!"

CHAPTER 4

December 29th

3:19 p.m.

It's dark in here. Moist. A perfect place to call a home. Unlike that inhospitable prison of liquid and plastic. No, this place is snug, soft against my parapodium as I slide my mouth and antennae through a slippery coating of wax and hair.

It's comforting. And yet, terrifying at the same time.

I use my palps to feel around, sensing the new and inviting space I've found myself thrust into. I use my body to slither down.

Mining deeper.

Curling through this twisted, fleshy corkscrew to the end.

Something is happening at the other half of me, and my head, which was once retracted within the safety of my body, projects out straight, spanning the length of what remains of me.

I smash against the walls around me, filling the space in a panicked explosion of movement as white-hot pain radiates through me.

It's pressure. Violent pressure.

And pain.

I'm being crushed, insides mashed. It's agony. The onset of panic ensues, but I won't give up without a fight. I simply cannot.

In a last-ditch effort to stay here in this inviting place, I writhe with the graceful fluidity I'm accustomed to and widen my proboscis, spreading it open with one fluid movement. In a fraction of a moment, I needle my teeth into the spongy end of this cavern and lock tight. I inject every drop of my coppery venom into the meaty substance in hopes that it will immobilize the offender.

But it doesn't help.

I must hang on. I must not scream. Or that will mean the end of this place. And possibly the end of me.

All five of my hearts feel like they are beating out of me.

I feel myself tear apart.

I want to scream. I want to open my jaws and erupt with a sound I know will not come. A sound that wouldn't change anything, even if it did. Damn this silence.

I have to get deeper.

I feel my insides crunch and shred. I feel tissue tearing, organs separating. My blood glugs out into this new comforting locale that I refuse to leave.

My lower half separates from me, and I am now nothing but a toothy proboscis and a few shorn segments. Just beating hearts, a stomach, fleshy organs, and sacs, all askew. My mushy, damaged insides trail out of the shorn end of my lesser segments. I am just a squirming mass of tender, twisting meat and legs.

Excruciating waves of pain flow through what's left of me. My phantom lower-half thrashes as if I'm willing it with my mind. I can't let go.

The pain and fear quell after a moment. This dull, throbbing ache washes over me again, but I can already feel myself starting the process of regrowth. I feel my miraculous body healing itself. I gnash my mouth, tunneling through the soft wall in front of me, from the darkness into the further unknown.

It only takes a moment before I am through, tucking my shortened body through the hole I've made, burrowing into a place of safety. Into a wet abyss. My fear begins the slow task of subsiding within me, and all I want is to sleep.

I have all of the time in the world now.

Hundreds of thousands of hours ahead of me, just like those in the past. Now, on an expedition to a place of safety, I squirm and gnaw into the colorless matter beyond, savoring its delectable scent and burying my body in the constrictive folds of this bizarre new locale.

As I burrow into a comforting nook and drift off to sleep, the last thought I have is how lucky I am. Not just to be alive but to have stumbled upon a palace that seems to me to be a perfectly hospitable place to lay these eggs.

CHAPTER 5

December 29th

4:42 p.m.

ENNNNKKK!

The doorbell buzzed obnoxiously, like the nightmare version of some horrible game show.

ENNNNK, wrong answer!

Garrett flopped his head back in his chair, feeling the bones in his neck crunch together with audible pops. He felt dizzy at the sensation, equilibrium off after what that little asshole did to him. He stared at the water-stained popcorn ceiling, certain it was no longer up to code. The model in his hand shook subtly as rage filled him. The sound drilled into his ear, still pinging with dull pains.

ENNNNNKKKK! The buzzer sounded again.

He blinked hard, wishing whoever was on the other end would go the hell away. He stared at the front door, glossed in runny layers of shit-brown paint.

He imagined opening the door to see Hamilton, neck in his father's clenched hand, being forced to apologize. Then he imagined smashing that little twerp's face between the door and jamb repeatedly until the kid was unrecognizably mangled.

EEEEEEEEEEEEEEEEEEENNNNNKK KK!

Garrett sighed, returning from his satisfying fantasy, and dropped the model parts again. He ambled over to the doorway and held the button down, growling into the intercom, "*What?*"

Silence.

Ringing silence that seemed to throb like murky sound underwater in his left ear.

Then, finally…

"Jesus, is that any way to talk to ya' best *friend, fuck-stick?*" The voice was male, gruff. "Open up. I come bearing gifts, you asshole."

Garrett sprung to life, suddenly overjoyed. He smiled as he slammed his finger on the button to allow access into the building.

***

"Duuuuuude!" Garrett said as he nearly bowled Mike over with a hug, which was quite a feat. "Look at what the cat dragged in!"

Mike was stocky and stout. Even though he only came up to Garrett's shoulder, he had at least fifty pounds on the man. His head was shaved smooth and bald, save for a closely-manicured patch of buzz-cut hair on the top of his head, some of which peeked out from beneath his white baseball cap. His eyes were intense, ringed like a lemur with a consistent lack of sleep. Garrett was pretty sure his bestie regularly partook in cocaine. A broad smile was plastered across his meaty cheeks, beaming a row of clean, white teeth beneath his sharp features.

"God, man, what's it been?" Mike's voice perpetually had gravel in it, like he was always just getting over a cold. His accent screamed Jersey with every word. "Fuckin', what, two… two and a half years?"

"Jesus, has it been that long?!" Garrett ran his slender hands through his short, dark hair, eyes shimmering gleefully at the man before him.

"Let's see, it was Trout. Atlantic City. Three-day run in August. They were in *Boulder City* last year in August, so yeah, it had to be the one before."

"That was a great show."

"Eh, it wasn't my favorite A.C. run, but we did get that forty-two-minute *Cheeser,* which was insaaaane." Mike stomped the snow off of his tennis shoes on the floor mat, and Garrett snapped into another gear suddenly.

"Oh my God, where are my damn manners, man? Come in! Sit! Take your coat off! Mi casa es, you know, *your* casa."

Mike nodded and waltzed in, dropping his backpack to the floor. Garrett swung the door shut behind him and walked to the fridge. "You want a beer?"

Mike grinned sheepishly. "You know the answer to that."

"Light beer, fatass?" Garrett teased.

"*WhaddoIlooklike*, I'm on some kinda *diet*? Like I'm some broad tryin'a watch 'er figure?" Mike pointed to his chest with both flattened hands. His accent was so thick he sounded like a caricature.

"Here." Garrett spun the twist-top for a Brooklyn-brewed lager and tossed it over his shoulder in the direction of the sink. It popped against the walls and surfaces of the tiny kitchen like an errant pinball before finally settling near the rat trap. He handed off the already-sweating bottle. Mike took it graciously, sitting in one of the wooden chairs around the table with a groan. He stared down at the plastic array of unpainted vehicular pieces and parts. "Oh, I didn't realize you still played with *toys*. My bad, shoulda' brought you one of my nephew's transforma's."

Garrett chuckled and cracked open a chocolate stout for himself. He pointed to Mike's bottle. "Att'l be $22."

"Jesus, what's 'dis, a 12-ounce can at *Red Rocks*?" He sucked back some of the beer, knowing Garrett was only kidding.

"My God, it's good to see you, brother. How ya been?" He smiled and turned his chair around, sitting backward in it. He pressed his chest against the backrest, and the scene suddenly made him feel nostalgic. Suddenly, it felt as if they were back in high school again, just two nerdy loners who became friends over a shared taste in music and cheap weed.

"Man, I've been good. I went and saw Mongoose at The Gorge this summer."

Garret gasps, "Oh my God, I *still* haven't seen a show there."

"Dude! What are you waiting for? That place is sick! This was what… my third time there." He takes a swig of his beer and looks at the label for a moment, studying it. "Mongoose was great, too."

"Yeah, I haven't seen 'em live yet, but I streamed one of their shows on the couch tour a while back, and their stage presence is unreal."

"You gotta see 'em. They put on one hell of a show. The last time I caught them, what was it… down in Memphis? *Nashville?* Had to be Nashville. They were *not* on their A-game. The bassist just had foot surgery, and I don't know, man, the set-list was just… it was sub-par, in my opinion. No frills. Nothin' fancy. No flavor to any of the songs from their new album…" His voice drifted off as he looked around, eyeing Garrett's place.

"Oh yeah, you haven't seen the new digs, have you?" He spread his arms wide, motioning to the cramped apartment around them.

"I didn't know you could *rent* a shoebox. Pretty… cool."

"This is Manhattan, baby. If you can dream it, you can do it," Garrett joked.

"Yeah, in Asbury, this would be called a closet." Mike giggled. "Where's your Christmas tree? You take it down already?"

"I barely got room for a futon in this place, much less a *tree*. If I wanna see one, I walk my cold ass down to Rockefeller Square."

"Whaddaya pay per month fa' 'dis place?"

"Mikey, you do *not* want to know." He took another hearty chug and put the beverage down again, rearranging tiny plastic wheels and CV joints with the bottom of the bottle. "So, to what do I owe this pleasure?"

"Well, I was gonna text ya', but then I think, *why don't I just drive up there and ask him in person?*"

"Ask me what?" Garrett rubbed his hands together playfully.

"You see, I was wonderin'," he paused, "if you wasn't doin' nothin' for the next few days, I was thinkin' maybe I crash here in ya' shoebox to ring in the new year."

"Of course, man. Happy to have you." Garrett didn't think for a second about how it meant he'd have to sleep on the floor just to give Mike the futon. He didn't hesitate with the cramped quarters or lack of privacy. They were friends, sure. But through the years they'd become more like *brothers*.

"You sure I'm not intrudin' on ya'?" Mike motioned to the table full of model pieces. "I mean, it looks awful lively around hea'. I can see you're in the middle of some important stuff."

"Shut the fuck up." Garrett laughed and kicked the seat of Mike's chair backward, nearly flipping him over. He grabbed onto the table just in time, swishing the contents of his beer and sloshing some of its contents from the bottle.

"Goddammit, you almost knocked me ova'!" Mike chugged the last half in one long gulp and slammed the bottle down on the wobbly table. He licked the foam from his recently shaved upper lip. "You're not even gonna ask me why I need to stay?"

"I already asked, a--hole!" He rolled his eyes and chanted like the question was rehearsed. "Fine. Why do you need to stay, Mike?"

A big grin crept onto Mike's soft face, and he reached his plump fingers into the pocket of the coat he'd slung over the back of the chair. He pulled out something white and rectangular. "Because someone got a three-night pass in the lotto earlier this year to see *Trout* at *Madison-Motherfuckin-Square-Garden* for New Year."

"You *didn't!*" Garrett was green with envy at the site of the tickets. Trout had been the jam band that united them all those years ago. They'd since made so many memories travelling to see the band and attending shows throughout the country. Garrett knew the tickets were ridiculously expensive, and a three-day pass was something you shouted to the moon and back about on the Trout message boards and social media sites. The shows were always sold-out within an hour of being announced at the start of the tour.

Mike might as well have been holding a golden ticket to *Willy Wonka's Chocolate Factory* in his hand.

Suddenly, with all the flair and flourish of a magician, Mike waved his hand and fanned the tickets, revealing six altogether. "Merry-damn-Christmas, you six-and-a-half-foot shit-stain. An' a happy new year!"

CHAPTER 6

December 29th

4:47 p.m

Mel Tredo's squad car slowed to a crawl behind a row of late afternoon traffic. The heater fought against the frigid chill that seeped in from outside.

Luca Han looked ahead from the passenger's seat at the stop-and-go traffic with growing impatience. He never had to deal with this sort of traffic back home. He wondered how many people died in the city from blocked ambulances and delayed police response. Each ripple of movement was followed by a short engine rev and a sudden stop only feet ahead.

Luca grumbled. "We coulda *walked* there by now."

A man in his thirties with flushed, pale cheeks and a man-bun of chestnut hair turned to look at them, then quickly looked away as he walked in front of their vehicle. His calf-length black trench coat dusted the grill as he wiggled through. He hopped on the sidewalk and pushed through a few tourists, faces all tilted up at the skyscrapers.

"You've *got* to be kidding me. You *saw* that, right?" Luca asked in utter shock.

The NCO snapped out of her locked focus, seemingly oblivious. "Huh? What?"

Luca's jaw dropped. "What do you mean *what*? That guy just *jaywalked* in front of our cruiser!"

Mel stared at him as if a third eye had sprouted from his forehead. "Are you serious? Where do you think you *are* exactly?"

Luca batted his eyes in confusion. "*America*. Where that's *illegal*."

"You gotta learn to pick your battles, Guppy. You're in New York." She rolled her eyes. "Manhattan. Home to about 1.6 *million* people. That's on a *bad* day. If you didn't realize this, it's almost New Year's, too. That means 1.6 becomes damned near 2.6 million. Conserve your tickets and your energy. We're gonna need it. Plus, we already radioed that we were *en route* to that last call."

Luca felt deflated. He sat back in his seat, trying to wrap his mind around someone brazenly committing a crime in front of him and then being ordered to look the other way.

Mel scoffed. "Where'd you say you transfer from again?"

"Mystic."

"Ahhh, Connecticut. That explains a lot." Mel nodded. "Don't they have an aquarium there or something?"

"Yup."

"Why the hell would you come to Hell's Kitchen then?"

"It's slow there. Not much crime. Sat on my ass all the time. Felt like I could do more good here, you know? That 1.6 million and all…"

"Oh God," Mel rubbed her caramel-colored forehead in frustration. "Of course, the Captain partnered me with a starry-eyed white knight. That fuckin—"

"I'm no white knight. I'm more like the Korean Chuck Norris," Luca protested. "I just want to make my time and effort count, not sit at the station seeing who can throw a paper airplane the farthest."

Silence.

"It's me, by the way. I developed a fold where the nose is bent and it just takes off."

Mel sighed. "Right. Well, you'll have all the excitement you can handle here. Theft, drug-addled transients, violent rapes, burglars, domestic disputes, murder, you'll have your pick. Last week, I did a wellness check and saw a ripe, old guy, *super* dead. Buck-naked, slumped on the toilet *Elvis-style*. Still can't get that stink out of my hair. Have you ever even *seen* a dead body?"

"Is this *Stand By Me*? Come on! Yes, I've seen a dead body." He plucked his phone from the surprisingly-deep pockets of his navy uniform pants. "Hey, Siri." The phone chirped in response. "Show me the article titled 'Mystic's Mischief Manager of 2023.'"

An Australian woman's voice eagerly responded, "Showing top results."

"Thank you, Siri." Luca offered up the handheld virtual assistant.

"Did…" Mel began, unsure if she should continue. "Did you just *thank* Siri? You know you don't have to *do* that, right?"

He flipped through the produced results to find the right article. "You'll see. When AI takes over, and tech becomes sentient, we'll see if it remembers who said *thank you* and who treated it like a slave."

She raised her eyebrows, turned her eyes back to the road, and silently mouthed: *okaaaaaaaay*.

He skimmed through the first few lines. He found the quote he was looking for and read it aloud:

"...Never before has Mystic seen such high citation rates, resulting in a drop-off of violations and reportable incidents. It's about sending a message to tourists and surrounding counties that, here in Mystic, we take our policing seriously. We want to keep our home idyllic. A place where you can work, live, and raise children without fear. We are here to keep Mystic mischief managed."

With feigned interest, Mel nodded. "Wow, so you're the alleged *Mischief Manager?*" Unable to contain her laughter, Mel laughed aloud. "I hate to be the one to say it, but *that is* a stupid nickname."

Luca sneered. He wasn't sure why her words stung as much as they did. Maybe it was because he was proud of his nickname, and now he was back to being a small fry in a vast sea.

Or maybe it was because he couldn't stop picturing how her curvaceous body would look outside of her uniform. His mind wandered to thoughts of her naked beneath the cheap bedding in the apartment he could barely afford, tousled blonde hair barely covering her breasts, softly moaning his name.

Luca flinched in his seat and chastised himself for fantasizing instead of focusing on the job. *He was a fucking Han, dammit.* His father's voice echoed in the recesses of his mind: *Hans get the job done!*

Suddenly, he snapped back to reality as Mel spoke. "Why are you looking at me like that? You got something to say? Just say it. Do you think I can't handle a few *mean* words from some rookie from Mystic? *Please.* Do your *worst.*"

Luca opened his mouth and shut it again. When he looked at her, he lost his nerve. It was only day one, and he wasn't sure if he wanted to choke her or kiss her.

Maybe both.

She muttered in a baby-like tone with a pout, "Why are you so mad? Because I hurt your *feewings*?" She nearly rammed the bumper of the red sedan ahead of them as it halted abruptly for another jaywalker. The driver stuck an arm out of the window and flipped them the bird.

"Sorry, my dude! Baby on board!" Mel yelled out the cracked window and waved apologetically.

The driver sped off, changing lanes without a turn signal.

Luca stared, slack-jawed. "Okay, now *that* was illegal. You saw *that, right?*"

"Yeah, Mr. *Eagerbeaver*. But we are en route. Can't go stopping every two seconds. We don't know what kind of call we are responding to. It can escalate quickly. Someone could be bleeding out while you're parked at the fucking side of the road writing your ten millionth ticket for breathing wrong."

"You just saw—"

"I just saw us almost *hit* the guy."

"That's on *you!* You were too busy busting my balls to pay attention!"

"Dude, you gotta *relax*. You're seriously gonna stroke out on your first day. Don't be the cop who tickets people for going two miles an hour over the speed limit. Please? Nobody likes that guy."

With a sigh, Luca turned toward the window and mumbled loud enough for her to hear. "I mean, it's called a speed *limit* for a reason, but fine."

"Alright, Officer *Try-Hard*," she added, lurching the vehicle sloppily into a narrow parking space and throwing the car into park. She pressed the button on her shoulder radio and turned her face toward Luca. "Dispatch, this is Unit 16."

"Unit 16, go ahead," the woman's voice chirped through mild static.

"Unit 16, responding to 10-50 at 341 West 49th Street. What apartment are we looking for?" She released the button on her radio and stared out the window at a group of kids walking by, kicking at the remnants of snow that capped the microscopic lawns.

"Unit 16, apartment 208. Responding to a one Rachel Ligerski. Single occupant. Unarmed neighbor dispute."

"10-84, just arrived." She released the button on her radio and unlatched her seat belt. "You can take the lead on this one, Guppy. I gotta see how much you need to unlearn."

Luca looked out of his window at the slush-lined curb her tires had ridden up on and sighed. "You know, *I* may be a *try-hard*, but at least I don't park like an *asshole*."

CHAPTER 7

December 29th
5:06 p.m.

Luca's mind was elsewhere as the elderly woman babbled in front of him. He looked over her shoulder into her apartment. Every surface was covered in crocheted doilies, papers, magazines, knickknacks, and other junk. A cross-eyed angel stared at him from her windowsill, silently judging their presence.

"He acts like he *owns* the damn place, what with all that clompin' around," the woman screamed in Luca's face. "Sounds like he's got a fuckin' horse up there trainin' for a race. And I done called you idiots multiple times now, and you shitheads ain't done nothin' about it!"

Luca turned his gaze back to her just as something furry darted behind her recliner. He said a silent prayer that it was a cat. A really *big* cat.

"I understand, Mrs. Ligerski—"

"*Miss,*" she interrupted. "My goddamn husband's *dead.* He used to be the one to fuckin' deal with idiots like that clumsy fuck upstairs. Him and my son. But you took him away, too, and left me some lonely spinster. It's clear you people won't do anything about that fat fuck upstairs. You're out here arrestin' people who don't deserve it and leaving assholes to run the damn streets! Now you two human-stains are just standin' in my fuckin' doorway lettin' the heat out insteada fixin' the fuckin' problem *yet again*!" She clapped her skeletal palms together in between the words: "Get… his… lard… ass… outta… here!"

Luca was stunned by the venomous poison spewing from the vulgar old woman. He amused himself by counting the cuss words; it *had* to be some sort of a record. He suddenly felt a pang of regret, momentarily missing the small-town feel of his old precinct.

"Unfortunately, *Miss* Ligerski," Mel clamped her eyes tight as she emphasized the prefix, "we can't just evict someone from their place of residence. If they get their mail here, and he's not threatening to harm you and isn't a danger to themselves or others, then there isn't much we can do during daytime hours except to ask him to keep it down. But you need to understand he doesn't *have* to. The noise ordinance isn't in effect until evening time."

"Are you kiddin' me?!" She threw her hands in the air and let them fall, slapping the sagging, bare thighs pouring out of her *I Love My Maine Coon* nightshirt. Both Luca and Mel prayed she was wearing something, *anything*, beneath it.

Luca didn't respond to the woman's outrage. Instead, he remained calm. "Have you spoken to your landlord?"

"That fuckin' moron always says he can't hear a damned thing because he's at the other end of the hall. I'm half *deaf,* and I hear *everything* this loud-ass *sonofabitch* does." She pointed a wrinkly finger up into the air. "I know he's doing this on purpose! It's like he's stomping around in tap shoes up there just to drive me crazy! What's the fucker doing? Reenacting *Stomp*?"

"*Feed me. Feed me. Feed me,*" squawked the African Gray Parrot, waddling back and forth, bobbing its head inside of the wire cage behind her.

"Shut up! You're on a damn diet, Pete, deal with it!" Ligerski shouted over her shoulder before once again returning her attention to the officers in her threshold.

"Have you considered *moving?*" Mel suggested, trying to contribute something other than being a pretty face for the old bag to screech at.

Ligerski reeled furiously, glaring at them both as if they'd just simultaneously slapped her in the face. She snarled at Luca and then at Mel. "Look here, you lazy-ass public *servants*. This place may not be fancy, but it's fuckin' *rent-controlled.* Do you think I can afford to give that up with this goddamn *inflation* hikin' up our ass? It's hard out there right now, and I sure as hell ain't made a' money. On my pension, I couldn't afford a crackerjack box in *Jersey* these days. I'm not leaving *my* home because some ass-hat has heavy feet! *He* should have to leave. Not me! I was here loooong before him."

Mel nodded to appease the old broad and then flashed a sideways glance at Luca. "Miss Ligerski, I assure you we'll go upstairs and ask him to keep it down."

"No," Ligerski vehemently shook her head. Her cheap, layered costume jewelry necklaces jingled together loud enough to nearly drown out her indigent tone. "Talking time is over. Arrest his ass. Throw him in a cell."

"For what exactly?" Mel scrunched her forehead, leaning forward with her arms crossed.

Above, heavy footsteps lumbered loudly, pacing back and forth. Aged floorboards groaned beneath the tenant's weight, drawing Mel and Luca's attention to the water-stained popcorn ceiling.

"Ya' hear *that,* officers Dumb and Dumber? For *what?* For *WHAT*?! For disturbing the *peace! My* peace! That *was* against the law, last time I checked."

"That only applies to making unreasonable noise. He's just walking around."

"So you're not gonna do anything? He might as well buy some size-fatass high *heels* and send me straight to the nut house!"

Luca and Mel looked at each other, both at a loss. Mel rolled her neck and straightened her posture, ready for round two with Ligerski. Luca's eyes briefly glanced down, his attention temporarily diverted to the way Tredo's breasts tugged at the buttons of her shirt. He caught a brief peek at her lacy pink bra and pinched his eyes closed, hoping the image would permanently stain his memory.

Focus Han!

He snapped back to reality, rattling off the first thing that came to his mind. "Miss Ligerski, I don't think he is doing it intentionally. Much of the noise has to do with the age of the building." Luca pointed to the floor. "Invest in a good set of noise-canceling headphones with the money you're saving on rent hikes. Maybe buy him some slippers as a peace-offering or a belated Christmas thing."

The look in Ligerski's haunting, steely eyes bore into Luca's. The sudden, unexpected silence between them sent a frigid ripple through his body.

"Buy… him… *slippers*?" Her neck skin wobbled like a rooster's wattle as she screamed. "You have to be fucking kidding me?!"

Mel took a step toward her, "Miss Ligerski, we need you to lower your voice."

Miss Ligerski balled her fists. "You donut-scarfing fuck-sticks never do a God-damned thing! *My* tax dollars pay *your* fucking salary! I'm *your* boss! Get your ass up there and *do* something!"

From the sidelines, Han fought the urge to snatch the old woman by her necklaces and twist them until she turned blue.

Beside him, Mel noticed Luca's stare and took action. Her voice startled him, booming louder and more commanding than he had anticipated.

"Ma'am, lower your voice! If you don't, *you'll* be taken down to the station and booked for *disturbing the peace*. Now, we are gonna go upstairs and have a chat with your neighbor, okay? We'll ask him to keep it down."

"I should have known you'd just waste my time *again*." Ligerski shook her head as the two left. As soon as they were clear of the frame, she slammed the door. Due to the age of the building, the latch didn't catch, and the door bounced out of the frame, flapping wide open again. Infuriated, Ligerski slammed her form against the door and latched it with the chain lock.

Luca stood stone-faced, unsure how the meeting had devolved so quickly. He was startled by Mel's sudden snort. She pinched her lips closed, struggling – and failing – to hide her laughter.

They stood in silence for a moment before the parrot chimed in again. *"Feed me!"*

Tredo's shoulders shook with muted laughter. "Ol' *Mischief Manager's* off to a bangin' start, if I do say so myself. I thought at one point you were gonna fist-fight the old bat."

Luca shook his head and stormed up the decrepit stairwell.

"Walk quietly," Mel teased, "or ol' Ligerski'll come and whoop your ass."

CHAPTER 8

December 29th

7:39 p.m.

The walk to Madison Square was usually brief and uneventful, but the presence of black ice slicks on the sidewalks and muddy slush in the nooks and crannies of the road slowed both men down substantially.

"What about *her?* She's cute." Mike stuck his red face out of the neck hole of his taupe zip-up jacket and then sucked it back in like a shy turtle, using the high collar as a face covering.

"*Who*-her?" Garrett asked, looking around. His ear throbbed. He was preoccupied with the pain and not paying much attention to his surroundings. He felt anxious about spending hours assaulted by noise but wasn't about to look a gift horse in the mouth. There were hundreds of people across the country that would give their hairy, right testicle to be doing a three-day stretch of Trout at MSG.

"The broad that just walked by." Mike popped up like a gopher again and then plummeted beneath, leaving exposed a

Rudolph-red nose and little else. "The fuckin' dumper on that broad. Jeeeesus Christ."

"The *dumper?*" Garrett jutted his head forward and laughed. "You're a pig."

"What the *fuck*, man? See, this is why you don't get any *trim*. It's like you're oblivious." Mike slowed.

Garret noticed and turned, halting his briskly-paced stride so fast that a man in a woolen trench coat nearly slammed into him.

"Ey!" The stranger hollered.

"Oh, shit. I'm sorry." Garrett instinctively grabbed the man's arm apologetically, then released and locked eyes. For a fraction of a second, Garrett scanned the depths of his mind to figure out if he recognized the man or if he only *seemed* familiar.

Without a word in response, the man breezed past, and Garrett's eyes followed him. He started to walk again and then finally looked over at Mike.

"Ohhhhhh." Mike smacked himself in the forehead. "It makes so much sense now!"

"What does?" Garrett faced forward and shivered, dodging a rippling puddle of watery grime.

"It makes sense. You're an attractive guy. Well-dressed, which, frankly, shoulda been my *first clue.*" Mike smiled at the realization.

"I don't understand what you're implying."

It was a lie. He knew *exactly* what Mike was insinuating.

"It's okay, dude, I'm an *ally* or whateva'. I just wish you coulda talked to me about it. I'm ya' best friend, and I've been tryin' ta set you up with girls, 'n whatnot. I coulda been helpin' you find ya'self a handsome fella."

"A *handsome fella?* What is this 1955? You're talkin' like you're in a black-and-white movie."

They waited at the corner with a mob of other bundled-up walkers, several of whom bolted across the street long before the *walk* sign flashed. The honking of the car horns never even registered to them. It was as if the vehicles were ghosts, crying out to be heard on a plane that New Yorkers weren't sensitive to.

"It's not a big deal. Not to me, anyway. I don't get it, but I, like, you know, *support* it." The way Mike said *support* in his Jersey accent made Garrett want to laugh. He sounded like he was getting punched in the family jewels, fighting the urge to vomit.

"What is it with everyone today calling me fucking gay? First, the little jerk next door to me, and now you. How is my sex life anyone's business?"

"Are you…" They walked for a moment. Mike seemed like he almost couldn't stomach what he was about to say. "That, *whaddathey* call that… *asexual*?" He made a comical expression of slight disgust as if he was pleading for Garrett to correct him.

"I'm not *asexual*. I love sex." Garrett zipped up the last two inches of his coat, fidgeting with the zipper as the colossal, dome-shaped venue came into view. "What I *don't* like is talking about my sex life."

"Alright, I'll drop it. Just know, I could be a good wing-man for ya' if you let me. Even if it's wit' the boys."

Garrett hooked his arm around Mike's thick neck and smiled. "I know, man."

"Alright, get the hell off me. I gotta get my ticket out." Mike grinned and shrugged him off, whipping his wallet out of his back pocket and plucking out the first night's ticket.

Soon, they'd made their way through security and up the comical amount of escalators. During the awkward silence, Mike leaned against the moving rail and looked at Garrett. "You take one 'a those pills I gave you?"

"Not yet. I was gonna take one once we got situated inside. I don't know how strong they're gonna be."

"Just start out with a half of one if you're drinkin'. Any more than that and it'll be lights out for yas. I don't need you sleepin' through the encore and I ain't carryin' your ass back to the apartment." Mike snickered.

"Thanks again for those."

"Hope they help. I keep 'em around for my back. They do help with the pain. Ya' gonna be," he clicked his tongue, squinted, and shot a finger-gun Garrett's way, "feelin' groovy, my man."

Garrett tried to smile but the throbbing in his ear made it look like the expression was made under duress.

"I can't believe that little prick did that to ya. Someone needs to beat his ass." Mike shook his head. "Want me to go over there tomorrow and lay the smack down, Asbury-style?"

"Shoot, I'll buy you ten beers if you do."

The duo reached the landing and snaked through the concourses, taking detours through the overpriced beer garden for a twenty-two dollar tall-boy that would normally be three bucks in a convenience store. They meandered to the merchandise booths, and impulse-bought New Year's limited edition shirts and holographic foil posters and took their spoils to head to their seats.

Once they were through the doors, the venue opened wide like a concrete-and-steel canyon. A smattering of die-hard fans were camped out on the floor below, some in costumes. Each wore glow-stick jewelry and tie-dye clothing and manually-inflated plastic opossums and beach balls that would soon be tossed around like a blowup doll at a bachelor party.

Garrett stared up at the bowed stack of amplifiers aimed right at him, dangling like a marionette from the steel trusses hooked to the steel I-beams above.

His smile faded as a dull ache radiated pain from his ear. He thought about the tinnitus-inducing blast of noise that would come out of those stacks.

This was going to be painful.

CHAPTER 9

December 29th

9:09 p.m.

The sound quakes me to my squishy core, and I feel the need to undulate and burrow. I can't seem to get away from it. I am weak from thrashing about, tunneling into the folds and creases of this soft, delicious matter. Despite having voraciously eaten a tunnel to these depths, I feel my health slipping away.

The trauma I endured is just too devastating.

As the sound pounds, vibrating the jellied matter around me, I decide that this place here, next to this tough structure, will be the best place to ensure the safety and viability of my children.

I must act now, or soon, I will not have the strength to do this.

There is no surface to swim to.

I've looked.

So, this gooey mound beside me will have to suffice.

I flex hard with the intact remainder of my body. I can feel the gametes release and slide from my mortal wound. I tense again, expelling them. Pushing. Broadcasting them around in the nooks and crannies. I watch them slip into the folds, cradled lovingly by the spongy, wet material all around us.

In my dying moments, I see them there...

Thousands of perfect, tiny eggs.

Each with its own chance to carry on my legacy.

CHAPTER 10

December 29th

10:45 p.m.

"Dude, you okay? You're all fuckin' sweaty," Mike screamed into Garrett's ear as he bobbed limply in place, off-beat. Garrett winced and yanked his head away so fast that he nearly head-butted the person to his other side, a middle-aged man in a Grateful Dead tee lighting up a stubby joint. He looked at the man and raised a hand apologetically, and then his eyes sluggishly drifted back to Mike.

Lasers tickled the audience, flitting light across Garrett's listless eyes.

"Seriously, dude. You look like shit. Have you eaten anything?" Mike hollered again over the jam-band's guitar solo.

Garrett shook his head.

Mike grimaced at how moist he looked in the colored lights shifting in the air above the stage. "Dude, maybe you should go get a burger or something on the concourse. You look like you're gonna pass out."

"I don't feel good," Garrett mumbled inaudibly.

"Huh? I can't fuckin' hear you, dude."

Garrett screamed, anger thick in his voice. "I don't fucking feel good!" He sighed heavily. The scream had drained him of almost everything. The pressure in his head made him feel like he was going to faint. He grabbed the seat of his chair to steady himself.

Mike stopped dancing and looked at him with concern. "Dude, I hate to say this, but maybe you should go home."

Garrett didn't want to leave in the middle of the show, but he feared if he didn't go soon, he might be leaving in an ambulance after a collapse. The thought of walking the sixteen blocks home was daunting.

As if he could sense what Garrett was thinking, Mike pulled out his wallet and whipped out some cash. He grabbed Garrett's arm and stuffed the money in his hand. He leaned in close and tried not to shout, though to do so, he nearly had to press his lips to Garrett's ears. "Take a taxi. Text me if you need anything, okay?"

Garrett stared at the money and reluctantly took it. He wrapped an arm around Mike and hugged him tight before nodding. Leaving his coat and gloves behind in his chair,

he clutched his injured ear and made his way
out to the aisle, squeezing past the drunken
fans all dancing in place.

CHAPTER 11

December 29th

11:23 p.m.

The gray tone of Garrett's once-vibrant skin echoed the soulless look in his eyes as he shuffled his way through the convenience store at the end of his block. He trudged through the too-narrow aisles like some kind of recently institutionalized housewife in an asylum. He looked docile and sickly, but inside, he felt the nauseating effects of rage percolating within him, coming to a boil.

As he made his way down to the can coolers of alcoholic beverages, his elbow caught a jar of strawberry preserves. The container fell, shattering to the floor in an instant grenade of red liquid and he stopped in his tracks. The intoxicating scent of sugar and berries filled his senses as if someone had maced his face with fruity air freshener. His eyes lit up at it.

"You have to buy that!" The young woman behind the cash register hollered, chewing a mouthful of bubblegum as exaggeratedly as a cow gnaws cud. She sighed and put her phone down on the counter.

Garrett squatted down to pick up the shards of glass.

"Don't step on it. Just leave it there. I'll clean it up in a minute." She scrambled around, looking behind the counter for cleaning supplies.

Garrett looked at her as if she were speaking another language. He narrowed his eyes, glaring at the young thing as she moved around behind a thick sheet of marred plexiglass, a remnant from the darker days of the pandemic.

She disappeared out of sight and, moments later, popped back up in his aisle like a surfacing gopher. Her hand was wrapped around the rough handle of an aged mop, one that had seen far better days.

The rollers of the yellow mop bucket dragged against the chipped squares of tinged linoleum with a *grnnnnnnn.*

POP!

A hellaciously-loud bubble exploded near her face, and she hungrily gnawed the deflated wad of white putty back between her teeth. The sound of her gum firing like a tiny canon juddered Garrett back to life. She ground her jaws, chewing hard.

She frowned at the mess of glass and preserves in his hand. He was mashing it, grinding it together between his fingers and along his skin, dead eyes aflutter with the sensation.

"Dude, what the fuck?" she barked.

He stood, slow and unsteady, rising as if commanded to his feet. He felt the pressure in his head pulsating, unaware that the larvae were writhing and active, making a meal of his amygdala with their hungry mouths and tiny, copper teeth.

"I said don't touch that."

"You said don't step on it."

"I didn't think I had to fuckin' *clarify*, asswad." She rolled her eyes and chewed.

POP!

The sound of her gum snapping nearly crippled him this time, driving a spike into his already injured brain with its sharp, sudden noise.

He clenched the shards of broken glass in his fist, feeling the way they made such quick work of his skin as the small shards burrowed inside of his palm and fingers.

"*Stop the popping.*" His voice was a whisper, threatening and low.

"What?"

"I said *stop*... the *popping*," Garrett warned again, locking his eyes on hers.

She wasn't afraid in the slightest.

"Why? Whaddaya gonna do about it, huh?" She spread her arms wide, unafraid. "You the fuckin' BubbleYum police or somethin'?"

She chewed again and eyed him, this time noting his *off* coloring. The yellowed sclera of his eyes. The compulsory twitch of his right brow. The tenseness of his jaw…

"You know what?" She mashed the wad between her molars some more and pointed up to the front counter. "Pay for the jelly and get the hell out of here. I don't want you in my store."

"*Your* store?" He laughed.

She noticed that he was sweating. Profuse beads of it ran along the wrinkled creases in his face. The white shirt he wore was soaked in both armpits. He looked like he'd just run three miles. His prematurely-slivering hair was matted to the sides of his face.

It was freezing out. It wasn't much better inside the store. The thought of walking around that sweaty without even a hoodie made her want to shiver just looking at him.

"Are you *sick*, dude? Because if you got some new variant, I ain't even," she waved her hands and didn't finish. "Nnn-nnnnn. No, thank you."

She took a stride backward and, without thinking about it…

POP!

Without so much as a second to let what she'd done register, Garrett launched himself at her like a fired cannonball. He leaped forward and palmed her face, using his height to his advantage as he smashed jam and broken glass into her eyes and smeared.

The attack caught her so off-guard that she barely let out a yip before they were on the floor, sandwiched by the narrow aisle's racks. He pressed harder, feeling a shard of jelly jar pierce the fragile casing of her eye.

She screamed.

Runny fluid oozed out like a broken egg yolk, and she flailed her limbs, reaching for anything she could.

"Stop!" She was screaming, pummeling the side of his face with over-inflated candy bars, ripping things off shelves.

He smeared his hand over her mouth, slicing her lips with the glass embedded in his own skin. His palm felt like it had built-in razor-blades, like some kind of fucked up X-Men reject. He held his hand across her face, and she could taste the warm, iron essence of his blood mixing with the shard-filled preserves on her tongue.

She grasped overhead, bringing the mop bucket down with a *sploosh* of rancid, black water, soaking her back and bathing his knees that had her locked into place. The mop came down with it.

She cried beneath the weight of him, shuddering with her suffocated pleas.

The sound of the noises she was making from the floor made his head pound like a bass drum with a repetition that drove him mad. He grabbed the soaked head of the mop with his free hand and examined its ash-gray coloring, once white. He released his grip on her mouth, and before she could get out a full scream, he smashed the stringed portion into her face, gripping both hands high up on the handle, forcing it down her mouth like he was plunging a stubborn turd. He pounded it down in her face, quieting her. Dark gray slop dribbled into her ruined cuts, mixing into a swirled broth before making its final descent to the floor.

The cashier clawed at Garrett's shirt, popping buttons, shooting them into the air like fleeing flying saucers.

She choked, waterboarded by the filthy liquid.

Her clawing grew weaker, but instead of letting up, he pushed harder, shoving the head of the mop down until he heard the sickening crack of her lower mandible freeing itself with yet another audible…

POP!

CHAPTER 12

December 29th

11:41 p.m.

Luca peered out from the passenger seat of the roaming white SUV as the strange city jogged by just beyond his window. Excited citizens filled with New Year's optimism shuffled in heavy gear, unfazed by winter's bite. Heavy, white clouds threatened to release another load of snow over the city at any moment.

The freezing temperatures made Luca wish he could turn on his heated seats, something the police patrol vehicles in Mystic had.

He didn't realize how good he'd had it.

The duo sat in silence. The only noise came from the hum of the vehicles around them mixed with the snake-like hiss of the underground subway system. Bustling citizens slithered past each other on crowded sidewalks.

Mel's huff finally broke the car's silence. "Are you seriously pouting?"

Luca straightened in his seat and stared, stone-faced, at the road ahead. "Not choosing to fight with my partner is not *pouting*. I am sorry if you see it that way."

"Those Connecti-cunts teach you how to gaslight like that in Mystic, too?" She swerved into an area designated for emergency vehicles and swiveled in her seat to face Luca. Her chocolate-colored eyes made his anger melt away.

How can you want to scream at someone and make out with them at the same time?

"Listen, you and I are havin' this out right here, right now. What is your fuckin' problem?" Tendrils of her pinned hair came loose from her bun with the force of her head bobs.

How could she be so pissed and somehow seem even more beautiful?

Focus, Han!

"You wanna know what my problem is with you? Fine."

Come up with something, Luca. Just don't tell her you're intimidated, living in an over-priced apartment where you're positive someone died of dysentery.

"I think you're one of those cops who tries too hard to be cool," Han finally said.

Mel recoiled, "What the hell are you talking about?"

"You're one of those cops that let too much shit slide, and people only do that for *two reasons*. One, either you're *lazy*, which I asked around, and you are *not*. Or, two, you're one of those cops who wants everyone to like them, so they let too much shit slide. We're not the New York welcoming committee. We're fuckin' NCOs. Frankly, if people wanna play stupid games, then they win stupid *prizes*."

A dusting of red appeared on her cheeks. "Are you finished?"

He swallowed hard and nodded.

Mel cracked her neck. "I'm ex-military. When I got stationed here with the army, I fell in love with this city. I'm not here to rule this place like a tyrant with a fuckin' badge. We got enough of those running around the streets making us all look like shit. I'm here to make sure people don't fuckin *kill* each other." She growled. "I'm not some ditzy pushover looking for drinkin' buddies. I'm here, *in the shit just like you*, tryin' to *serve and protect*. New York's got overflowing correctional facilities and a backlog of court cases so long it would make your head spin. So before you further cripple a buckling system with more unnecessary bullshit, just *think*."

Luca sat back, feeling deflated.

"I'll work on reeling myself in. But you need to lay off me, too. I'm not a perp or a suspect. Right now, I'm your partner. We could have talked about this over a hot dog or something. Don't keep laying into the one person who's supposed to have your back."

She faced forward and squeezed the bridge of her perfect nose. "Jesus, you're giving me a fuckin' headache."

"I tend to have that effect on women." Luca chuckled.

Mel laughed. "We good?"

Luca shrugged and nodded. "Until I piss you off again. Any other shit you wanna air out? Religious preferences? Political affiliations? Sport teams? Let's get all the dark shit out now."

"Agnostic, Independent, and Giants, even though they shit the fucking bed this season. *Again*. Now, how about you buy me that fuckin' hot dog now that you put the idea in my brain? I'm starving."

"Grey's around here?"

"It's outside our jurisdiction."

"By, like, what? A couple blocks?"

"Oh, goodie-two-shoes is a rule-breaker now?"

Luca stared at her, fighting the urge to smile.

"Fine. We can go. But *you're* buying. And I'm getting papaya juice, too, so just know that upfront."

"I'd expect nothing less."

As Mel was about to shift the car back into drive, she heard a voice come over the radio.

"Unit 16, come in."

Luca reached for the handheld receiver, and Mel quickly swatted his hand away. "Paws off my radio." She snatched it from the holder. "Dispatch, this is Unit 16."

"Unit 16, we've got a 10-24C. Woman called in from the Pop Shop at 412 West 49th Street. Cashier is in rough shape. Suspect at large, presumed armed and dangerous."

Han and Tredo glanced at each other. *Showtime.*

"We're *en route*, about 3 minutes out. Did the caller give any further information?"

"Good Samaritan called it in. Cashier's injured. Medical assistance required. Ambulance is five minutes out. They have to go around the parade on 10th Ave. You'll most likely beat 'em there."

"10-4." Mel clamped the receiver back on its rest and threw the car into drive, blipping the sirens briefly to get people to move. She looked over at Luca and pointed. "Don't think I'm forgettin' about that fuckin' hot dog."

***

"Sh-should we check for a pulse?" Luca's face, drained of all color, gaped at the horrific scene before him. From where they stood at the end of the aisle, the grizzly carnage was all too clear. The unmoving victim was sprawled like a gore-covered starfish. Her face, or rather, what was *left of it,* was gouged and coated in viscous blood. A devastated eye socket glimmered with a mix of clear fluid and a wad of optical nerves from the ruptured orb, like a camera that had been ripped from a wall, cables dangling.

Her jaw hung unnaturally, the bones shattered and dislocated. The mop's handle laid down the length of her, and the filthy head was draped around the sides of her throat.

Murky, red tendrils of it lingered inside her ravaged mouth. Several smashed-in teeth floated like gleaming-white vegetable hunks in the thick, red stew cooling in the back of her throat.

Down the aisle was a shattered jar of jam with prints of pink sludge tracked toward the body, disappearing beneath the watered-down sanguine pool that had formed like a halo around the clerk's head. Wet, ruby fingerprints speckled the floor and shelves.

"She's dead, Han."

"B-but shouldn't we *try* to save her? Maybe—" Luca stepped toward the body.

Mel tugged him back. "This is a crime scene. We need our booties and rubbers on. We can't risk ruining any of the evidence this sick fuck left."

"But she could be…"

"She's gone, Han. Took us 6 minutes to get here because of the fuckin' parade conjestion. She'd be brain-dead after four with no oxygen. That's not even countin' the time it took for someone to find her. Go get a witness statement from the guy who found her."

Luca forced himself to pry his eyes away from the body. An overwhelming feeling of nausea washed over him. He suddenly found himself gagging.

"Han, you toss your cookies *outside*," Mel barked.

Luca staggered to the door, bile biting at the back of his throat. He whipped the door open and felt the frigid winter air soothe his urge to vomit. He sucked in a few deep breaths and pinched his eyes closed. In the darkness, he saw the woman's body, oozing, dribbling. He saw her horrified, deformed face contorted in a forever-scream of pain, her only intact eye locked on the stained ceiling tiles. He opened his eyes and gritted his teeth.

"Either go out or come in, Han. I can't have the wind blowing shit around in here."

Luca nodded and closed the door, catching a whiff of the metallic scent of blood and cleaning chemicals.

"You keepin' it down?" Mel's look of genuine concern was etched across her features.

He nodded and motioned to the man in the back. "Yup. I'll… go get that statement."

Blue-and-red lights flickered brightly through the window of the cluttered convenience store, shielded by cigarette ads and a peg board labeled BANNED with printed low-definition photos of shoplifters. Luca studied it.

Tredo was still squatted near the mop handle and followed his line of sight to the board. "Those stills are pulled from a security cam. If it was recording, that'll make this shit a whole lot easier."

Han's head whipped around, looking for the location of the mounted equipment, finding it angled toward him from the back-left corner of the store.

He flashed a serious look at Mel and pointed at the camera, "Bingo."

CHAPTER 13

December 30th

1:31 a.m.

"You were right!" Tredo waved a printed black and white photo in the air. "Got the sick fuck, right on candid camera." Despite the gore around her, a smile crept up at the corner of her lips.

Han uncrossed his arms and held his hand out for the photo. "Let me have a look. Do you recognize him?"

"Nope." Tredo handed over the photo, looking back at the aisles, now cordoned off with signature canary-yellow crime scene tape.

"He looks pretty tall compared to these display shelves, and his shoe print's gotta be about a size twelve or thirteen."

"You know what they say about guys with big feet." Tredo bobbed her manicured brows a few times.

"Yep. Big shoes."

Tredo laughed a little at Han's stupid joke.

"I'm not seeing any tattoos or major scars. Did you see anything on the video?" Han asked.

"You mean other than this lady getting brutally beaten to death? *That'll* be living rent-free in my head for a while." Tredo sucked air between her teeth at the replaying of the senseless brutality in her head. "He had a white button-down on. Looked like a sweaty banker."

"Well, hopefully, the detectives pick somethin' up on him. Maybe his fingerprints'll hit. Who knows."

"The M.E. just arrived. CSI is over there right now taking prints and pictures. Detectives kicked me out of the room. Shit's above my pay-grade. Never hurts to be nosey though, I guess."

"Seems like it'd be a great way to piss people off," Han replied.

"Gotta step on a few toes when you're learning to dance with the big boys."

"You wanna be a homicide detective now?"

The question forced Tredo to think for a moment. "Nah. Well, *maybe*. I like the beat. I like getting to know people. Talkin' face-to-face. I like sorta bein' the first line of defense. Detectives have a lot more red tape. I fuckin' hate red tape."

"What next?"

"Next, we wait for everyone to clear out, then we lock it up and observe from the squad car for a bit in case the perp returns to the crime scene."

"Great. I gotta spend the night in the car with you disrespecting Siri and listening to whatever the hell that trash was in the car earlier," Han teased.

Tredo looked back at him and smiled. "What? You don't like *Trout*? They are the single greatest jam-band of all time."

"Look around and see if this place has any earplugs, would ya? If I gotta listen to a night of twenty-minute off-key songs, I'll envy our corpse here."

CHAPTER 14

December 30th

3:18 p.m.

Garrett walked into the quaint guitar store and the tiny bell rang out, tinkling through the little shop.

"Hello?"

Jerome walked out of the back, flashing his brilliant, bleach-white smile. "Oh man, am I glad to see you." He rolled his eyes as if to say: *It's been a day.*

Jerome rushed over to the door in long, graceful strides. He looked outside suspiciously and grabbed the plastic hanger on the back of the glass door. He adjusted the miniature clock hands on it and flipped the *back in 10 minutes* sign so that it would face toward the street. He twisted the key in the lock with a *clink*, grabbed the front of Garrett's shirt with his dark fingers, and dragged him to the back of the long, narrow store.

Halfway to the back, Jerome stopped and spun toward him, smiling. He looked down at the bandage on Garrett's hand.

"What'd you do? Lose a fight with a paring knife again?"

"Oh," Garrett pulled his hand away and laughed. "Something pretty much just as stupid. Broke a dang jelly jar." He looked down at the cuts, rubbing his thumb along the rougher, healing ones on the pads of his fingers. He scanned his mind for any remorse for the brutal act but came up empty, as if drained of all empathy.

"Aww, my poor baby." Jerome kissed him on the lips. Garrett kissed him back passionately and then pulled away and smiled.

"Mmmm, it's good to see you, too."

Garrett leaned up against the glass counter, sighed heavily, and rolled his neck, trying to crack it. "It's been a rough twenty-four hours."

"Yeah? What happened?" Jerome cocked his head to the side, and it reminded Garrett of a chocolate lab.

"Remember that asshole kid that lives next door to me?"

"The Broadway kid?"

"Yeah, *that* little dickhead."

Jerome's smile faded and morphed into a slight frown.

"*What*?"

"It's just, I have rarely heard you cuss before. In fact, I'm not sure I *ever* have. Your vocabulary is always so… PG13."

"I'm sure I've cussed in front of you before."

"No, no you haven't."

"Anyway… his dad asked me to come over and babysit him for a little while yesterday, and while I was napping on the couch, the little shit-stain put a fucking *worm* in my ear."

"He did *what*?"

"He stuck a worm… in my *earrrrrr*," he exaggerated the word, "when I was *sleeping*." Garrett shuddered at the thought as it replayed in his mind. "I coulda knocked the little asshole out!"

"Have you seen a doctor?"

"No, I called. Primary care said my doctor can't get me in until next week and it's not like I can afford to go to the fucking *emergency* room. Besides, I think I got it all out."

"Wait, you *think* you got it out? You're not *sure*?"

"It looked like it was cut in half when I threw it on the floor."

"Baby, I — " Jerome caressed the side of Garrett's face lovingly.

"Hey, c'mon!" Garrett thrust himself, using the countertop to launch. "Quit worrying about it, *okay*? Goddamn." He growled and balled his fists. "Jesus Christ, I don't need a *mother* right now. I just came in to see how you are doing."

Jerome frowned and wiped something off the counter, hurt by the exchange.

"Oh, come on. Don't pout," Garrett snapped.

Jerome was taken aback. Garrett had always been so *meek*. So *loving*.

None of it made sense. It was like a whole different person standing before him.

"Maybe you should go." Jerome scrubbed the glass harder with the sleeve of his Rolling Stones hoodie.

Garrett rolled his head again, this time cracking his neck like acorns under a tire. He peered into Jerome's eyes.

"I'm sorry." His tone was disarming, he plunged his hands into his jacket pocket and nervously fidgeted with one of the loose pain pills Mike had given him, nearly wearing off the coating with his scabby fingertips.

Jerome relaxed his body a little, visibly relieved by the apology.

"I'm just stressed. Mike's in town right now, too, and I —"

"Mike… as in your friend from Jersey, Mike?"

Garrett nodded. "He's crashing at my place for the weekend."

He could see the flicker of jealousy in Jerome's brown eyes like a candle in a breeze.

"Are you and he…?"

"Oh, GOD no. Are you kidding me? I'd rather go *straight*. Trust me, babe. He is not my type." Garrett leaned in and stroked Jerome's face with a smile. "Besides, why would I possibly need anyone else when I got you?"

Jerome's cheeks rose bashfully, and he lifted his shoulders in an awkward shrug. Garrett leaned in and kissed him again, softly at first and then leaning in with more intensity.

Jerome pulled away and smiled. He looked around, eyes landing on the locked front door for a moment before returning to

Garrett's face. "I thought you weren't into PDA."

"I'm not. But," Garrett looked around and grinned, "I don't see anyone *here*, do you?"

"I mean, it's a glass door…"

Before he could say another word, Garrett was pressing into him again, nibbling his neck, hands sliding into the crotch of Jerome's tight jeans. Jerome gasped, face hot, eyes fluttering. He pulled away, feeling the sudden burst of blood rushing to his dick like a freight train.

"Stop. *Stop*," he giggled. "I have a business to run."

Garrett wiped his lips and stepped back, holding his hands in the air in surrender. "Alright, fine. *Tease*." He drummed his fingertips on the countertop as Jerome made his way behind it, trying to hide his growing erection.

"So what are you and ol' Mikey up to tonight?"

"Well, he actually showed up yesterday with a three-day pass to go see Trout at MSG. I couldn't believe it, actually. Those tickets are fucking impossible to get."

"Oh," Jerome made a slightly disgusted face and then over-corrected back into a fake smile as if pleased with the news, "is that the jam-band-thingy that you and he are all into?"

Garrett didn't laugh.

The comment actually enraged him and he wasn't totally certain *why*.

He tried his best to dial back his anger. "Yes," he hissed, "it's that *jam band thingy I'm into*. Tonight is night two. That's actually why I came."

"*Oh*." Jerome felt the sting of the innocent comment and silently cursed himself for being so emotional.

"Yeah, my head was pounding all through the show last night. Something about loud sound in the ear where that little cocksucker fucked with me."

Jerome fought to keep his jaw from dropping. He'd never heard Garrett speak with such crassness. It wasn't the words themselves. It was that the whole thing was so out of character for someone he thought he'd known well.

"You sell any of those hear-through earplugs for the loud sounds?"

"Yeah, the concert ones?"

"Yeah, exactly. I need some."

Jerome rushed to the back, eyes scanning the rotating racks in the cramped store until he found a pair. "They're not cheap. They're like $40, but they work great."

"Can I just borrow them and, like, give 'em back after New Year's?"

Jerome laughed.

…Until he realized Garrett wasn't joking.

Jerome scoffed. "What? So I can sell your ear wax to the next guy? I think not."

"What about whore credit?" Garrett asked flirtatiously, leaning over the display and splaying his hands out like a stretching cat. "I mean, a *store credit*?"

"No, man, I got a business to run. I can't afford to be giving away $40 hear-throughs. The Christmas season *sucked* this year for sales and now it's way slower. It's not like anyone's even knocked on my door since you've been in here."

"*I'll* knock on your door." Garrett bounced his eyebrows.

"What has gotten *into* you?" Jerome furrowed his brow. "Usually, I'm the one always pawing at *you*. You're like… did someone slip you a Viagra or something?"

"No! You just look really sexy right now."

"—And you don't have any money."

"What if I pay you back tonight?" Garrett leaned in.

The thought of Garrett lunging at him moments before made Jerome's heart race all over again. "What do you mean?"

"Well, what if you came over after the show?"

"And?"

"And… I pay you back for these *several… times… over.*"

"I thought you said Mike was staying with you."

"Yeah, you can meet him. I'll introduce you."

"What, like, as your *'friend from college'* or something?"

"No." He wrapped his arms around Jerome and pulled him close. "As my fella."

"Your fella, huh? Is this real life, or is this some kinda mob movie from the nineties where women are still called dames?"

Garrett ignored the question. "Then… after he goes to sleep…" He slid his hands beneath Jerome's hoodie, touching the dark skin of his lower-abdomen.

Jerome shivered.

"I can show you my appreciation." Garrett's voice was all but a whisper now.

"What if I'm too loud? You *know* how I can be." Jerome shyly smiled.

"Mike sleeps like the dead." Garrett grinned and neared Jerome's face. He pulled the package of hear-throughs out of Jerome's hand and dangled them in front of him. "Plus, if we're being too loud, I know *just* what to give him."

Jerome laughed.

"Plus, that little fuck next door was *just* saying how I never get laid." Garrett's look was mischievous.

"*Let's give 'em somethin' ta' talk about*," Jerome sang.

"Indeed. *Let's.*"

"Fiiiiiiine." Jerome giggled like a child. "What time?"

"Show gets over around 12:30. Should be home by 1:00."

"*A.M.*?" Jerome shouted. "Garrett, I'm an old man. I can't be *startin'* my night at 1:00 A.M."

"We can have a *sleepover*."

"Ooooh. We haven't had one of those in a while."

"So it's settled then?"

Jerome nodded and then covered his smiling face with his hand. "Boy, you are gonna be the death of me."

Garrett reached around and smacked Jerome's ass playfully and then headed to the door. He held the earplugs up in the air and sang, "*Thank youuuu.*"

"Flip the sign on the way out."

"Yep." Garrett changed the sign to OPEN and unlocked the door. "Later, handsome."

Jerome blushed and looked away, fighting the urge to grin at the sexual attention.

On the sidewalk outside, Garrett stuffed the noise-dampening earplugs in his jeans pocket and tossed the package into the over-stuffed trash receptacle.

The dull ache was back, full force, radiating waves of mild pain from his ear. The normal sounds of Manhattan seemed amplified ten-fold. The honking, the revved engines, the roil of the subway beneath them seeping through street grates… it all made his head throb.

CHAPTER 15

December 30th

4:15 p.m.

In the locker room back at the Midtown North Precinct, Luca's mind whirled with gory mental snapshots, each depicting some element of the crime scene at the convenience store from the night before.

The young woman's broken jaw.

The blood-filled gouges on her face.

The front teeth floating in her throat.

The look of terror plastered on her ruined face.

Clearly, it had been a frenzied attack. Unplanned. Chaotic.

The image of her punctured, dangling eyeball, like a split grape on a bloodied stem, made his stomach lurch.

Lost in thought, Luca was startled by the painful sting of an overzealous slap on his back.

"Morning, Han. Heard you were hiding out here," Mel teased. She plopped on the worn wooden bench beside him and noted the bags under his bloodshot eyes. "Hello? Earth to Han? Ugh, you look like shit."

Luca's gaze was transfixed on a red speck in the confetti'd epoxy floor, reminding him of a drop of the woman's blood. His mind shot back to the bloody fingerprints on the white tile floor.

Mel waved her hand in front of his face. Luca seemed to stare straight through it. "Han, what the fuck? You're a million miles away."

"*Why?*"

"Why what?" She fired back, making a sour face.

"Why *her*? Why that *particular* convenience store? It wasn't robbed. Cash was still in the register. He didn't even care about leaving fingerprints… or footprints. He just fucking… *brutalized* her."

"You're still stuck on *that*, huh?" Tredo snickered callously.

That got Luca's attention. "What the hell do you *mean*? Are you *not* still stuck on that? You didn't lose a wink of sleep last night over that fucking *horror show*?"

"We aren't medical examiners. We aren't CSI's. We're beat cops. We take calls. We arrive first. We protect the scene. We take

witness statements. We write reports. Then…
we dust ourselves off and start each day anew.
That's what we do. That's how we survive.
That's how we have any kinda longevity in
this career. That's all *we* can control."

"How can you be so *cavalier* about this?
A person fucking *died*."

Mel frowned. "People die every day, Han.
Some in more horrible ways than others. One
died, but the other million-and-a-half *need*
you." She scrubbed the floor with her shoe. "*I*
need you."

Luca felt his melancholic heart leap.
"Yeah?"

"Yeah. Because if you aren't here, they're
gonna stick me with *Fisher*. I hate that guy. He
has no sense of humor, and his coffee breath is
fucking *rancid*." She winked.

Luca chuckled.

A pale, redheaded officer rounded the
corner and jumped like a frightened cat. He
clutched the towel around his waist, skin still
glistening from the shower.

"What the fuck, Tredo! Captain told you
to stay the hell outta here. What if I was
walking around with my dick out?"

"Your dick *is* already out," Mel fired back. "It's that fuckin round thing on your shoulders."

"Fuck you," the startled cop snapped back.

"You wish, O'Brien." Mel Tredo rose and waltzed past O'Brien. "Han, let's roll."

Luca snatched his duty belt and followed Tredo out.

CHAPTER 16

December 30th

10:52 p.m.

The ache in his ear refused to subside, growing with intensity from the sounds of the band blasting through the amp stacks in spiderwebs of steel truss, hung with precision by trained stagehands. Garrett's eyes studied them, wishing he could climb them like ladders to rip apart the amplifiers with his bare hands one-by-one.

Mike waved Garrett closer, motioning for him to lean in. Garrett winced, knowing Mike would have to shout to be heard over the music.

And shout, he did.

Mike's voice bellowed right into the noise-dampeners, a device that wasn't doing much to numb the throbbing pain in his head and ear. "I gotta take a piss, dude. Make sure no one kicks over my beer. This was twenty-two-fuckin-dollars," Mike hollered with a gust of hoppy air summoned straight from his diaphragm.

Garrett nodded, flexing his fists in pain.

Mike disappeared, mashing through the laughably-narrow rows to the main staircases leading into the concourse.

The man on the other side of the gap leaned in to talk. "Is this *Back on the Plane*?"

Garrett didn't quite hear what he said but nodded anyway.

The man listened momentarily and then leaned in again, this time much louder. He touched Garrett's shoulder, gripping the over-priced Trout hoodie he'd purchased with the last of his cash until payday at the merchandise booth an hour before.

"Oh no, wait, it's *Papa Dance*! They must have just *teased Back on the Plane*!"

Garrett whipped his shoulder away, wiping the traces of draft beer from the cotton fabric with a scowl.

"Dude, what's your problem?" The guy spread his arms wide, nearly hitting someone dancing in the row above him with his lit joint. He took a puff of it, eyes locked on Garrett. The cherry glowed red-hot. "Look, I'm sorry, man. I'm just excited! I haven't seen these guys since Atlantic City back in September. I've been jonesin'." He hopped in place like an excited kangaroo and then offered the roach to

Garrett like a smoldering peace offering. "Here, man, you want a hit?"

Garrett felt rage boil in him at every sound, every vibration, every nudge of someone's shoulder in the claustrophobic space. The world felt unstable, and nausea crept into his beer-steeped belly insidiously, like an intrusive, grasping hand.

Unable to take any more, he abandoned his seat and mushed past the stoner. His eyes danced from the undulating stage lights to the fireworks-like display of glow sticks exploding in a burst overhead, thrown by excited fans by the fistful.

He ping-ponged through the tight aisle, feeling the ground sway, surging like a concrete trampoline beneath his soles as thousands danced hopelessly out-of-sync to the upbeat tune.

***

Garrett rushed into the bathroom and plunged his face into the basin of the first sink he came to. He held his trembling hands in front of the sensor and splashed cupfuls of water into his color-drained face. He looked at his reflection in the mirror, shocked by the pallid golem staring back at him. He looked sickly, sweating…

And that *pounding.*

God, that *pounding* in his ear!

"Hey-a, little *help*?"

Garrett twisted to face the stalls. One was cracked, with a pair of brown eyes peering through the gap. "Hey man, those fuckin' nachos on the upper concourse fucked my stomach up, and this stall's outta toilet paper. Mind helpin' a brother out and grabbin' me some from the next? I asked the attendant. He went looking for some more rolls, but that was like five minutes ago. I'm missin' the whole damn set!"

Garrett glowered at him, disoriented and angered. It was as if the man was speaking another language. He was having a problem comprehending the meaning of the man's words, as if all speech-recognition was glitching out in his brain.

"Uh, *habla... en-englais*," the man asked, butchering the Spanish words.

"I speak English," Garrett said finally, nodding as if in some kind of surreal dream.

The man leaning forward on the crapper exhaled with relief.

Garrett took a step and wobbled as if intoxicated, catching himself on the sink just in time.

"Woah, buddy. You okay? You don't look so good."

Silence.

"Shrooms? You trippin' on shrooms?"

Garrett shook his head but quickly wished he hadn't. The simple movement threw him off balance. He was unbelievably dizzy, experiencing the worst, most sudden, case of vertigo of his life.

It felt like a fistful of cooked spaghetti was twisting inside his head. Like the strands were writhing in unison, all part of one ropy mass.

He felt pressure in his ear, too, like a man's bent knuckle trying to force its way out of the snail-shaped orifice from the inside. He pulled out the noise-dampener earplugs to relieve the pressure. A small, red worm dangled from one of them, latched onto the silicone bulb with it's tiny, copper teeth.

Its body shot forward, doubling in size, ejecting the extension from inside itself like a minuscule erection launching from a garnet foreskin.

Garrett shrieked in terror and flung the plug at the tiled floor as if it were on fire.

The guy on the toilet wrenched his face into a soured expression of disgust. "Ewww, what the *fuck*, dude?!" He covered his mouth in horror. "Something just came out of your ear. Looked like a fuckin' *worm*!"

Garrett dropped to his knees and puked. The wave of noxious bile and foamy IPA displaced the worm, squirming on the floor. The beer pushed it like a rushing tide, thrusting it out to some unseen sea. It wriggled in the beige stew several feet away.

Garrett hyperventilated, gasping and wheezing, eyes wide with shock, unable to look away from the nasty thing that just came out of him.

…Something that was, moments ago, *inside of him.*

He felt the sudden, overwhelming urge to cough. He hacked like a dog on all fours, dry-heaving over his puke.

"Dude, I'm comin'." The man shouted from the stall, rustling his clothes in a flurry. "I'm ruinin' my *drawers*, but I'm comin'!"

The hacking continued until…

Garrett halted, eyes bulging, blood pressure sky-high, heartbeat slamming around inside of his skull like a caged monkey frantic to escape its confinement. He had been plunged into a living nightmare.

Barf soaked the bandages on his hands. His face was caught mid-cough in a frozen gag. He reached his trembling, puke-soaked fingers into his mouth and tugged out something…

Something long.

It felt stuck in one of the small holes in the back of his throat, near his nasal passages. He reached in and grabbed it, pulling carefully.

The look of terror on his face grew with every inch that slid out. Once it released its feet and teeth, he dangled it like a red linguine noodle in front of his tear-filled eyes.

Its head protruded, shooting like a mushy nesting doll out of one end of itself. Its tiny mouth with four needle-like fangs latched onto the meat of his thumb. With eyes unblinking, showering tears of absolute terror, Garrett watched the squirming worm try to burrow into the hole it was gnawing in his sliced-up fingertip.

The man fumbled with the waistline of his pants, scuttling forward. "You okay, ma—"

He took a wrong step, planting a tennis shoe fully in some upchuck.

BAM! He caught the slick puddle of vomit and launched forward, arm outstretched like Superman as he landed in the acidic brine, right on his ribs.

"God dammit," he howled, clutching his side and rolling further in the chunky saliva-soaked muck. "*Ahhhhhhhh!* Fuck! I think I heard something crack!"

The man tried to roll over and get up on all fours, but the pain was too great. He grabbed at his side and wailed in agony. "Don't just sit there… get help, man! Jesus Christ!"

But Garrett's eyes were affixed to the worm, writhing in liquid near the man's feet. The pain in his head surged, and the man's cries were infinitely louder without the earplugs in now. Every moaned decibel infuriated him more, and he could only see the injured man before him through the pulsing red vignette.

"AHHHHHH! Fuck!"

They were the last words to ever leave the man's yowling mouth.

Garrett grabbed the man's head in both palms. "Shut up!"

It was like a dream for him. His hands were not his own. Every time he slammed the screaming guy's face into the tile floor, it was as though he was playing a video game, disconnected from the reality and brutality of his actions.

He watched front teeth scatter, rolling like tiny dice into the grouted cracks. *Yahtzee*!

Through the ruby frame of viewing, he saw his hands doing things as if on autopilot.

He saw himself dragging the man back into the stall from whence he first came. He saw his fingers prying the man's damaged jaw apart, unable to feel the bites and cuts from the man's jagged, remaining teeth as he pressed the hollering man's top jaw to the front lip of the toilet.

Like a slow woodpecker pounding in his ear, he could hear the *click-click-click* of the man's bottom row of chompers as they clacked against the porcelain.

The man mumbled and cried, no doubt trying to plead for his life. Beneath his face, blood and black shit mingled in the toilet bowl in a foul concoction that smelled even worse than it looked. His hands fumbled and flailed, scratching and clawing at Garrett. But Garrett wrangled each of the man's wrists in his fists and wrenched upward, sliding his knee onto the back of the man's head.

The man cried for his life, blubbering between wet strings of crimson drool and shrieks of terror.

But Garrett had to silence him.

In a fluid motion, he pulled the man's arms back and lifted the pressure from his knee, dragging the man a foot away from the bowl like a broken marionette. He let gravity force them both down, smashing the man, mouth first, into the bowl. He heard bones in his face crack, and the screams swelled louder, amplified by the rounded mini-auditorium that the container of nacho waste and gore made.

Garrett did it again, pulling the man higher off the bowl and driving his face down again.

Over and over. *Smash after smash.*

Until the noise finally stopped. The man shuddered in his grasp, then let out a final exhalation of air before relaxing limply.

Garrett stumbled back, relieved that the noise had finally ceased, and dropped the man like a blood-soaked rag doll onto the tile. Huffing and puffing, out of air, he surveyed the scene and then turned toward the door, stamping garnet-and-puke footprints along his path.

As he exited, on the other side of the bathroom, he could hear another man shout from the entrance, "Oh--oh my God… fucking… *what?*"

When the man screamed, Garrett was already lost in the sea of tie-dye, swimming with the schooling stream of Trout-heads toward a doorway marked STAIRS. He zipped his black hoodie and darted through the door, enjoying the calm silence of the stairwell as he made his way down.

CHAPTER 17

December 30th
11:36 p.m.

In his toothpaste-spackled mirror, Garrett looked himself over. He took off his spattered black hoodie and tossed it in the tub. He examined the crisp, white button-down shirt beneath. The docile formality of it clashed with the intense rage which was still shredding his insides into ribbons like a wild Tasmanian devil. He rifled through the drawer of his sink, eyes flitting back and forth between its contents and the crimson smears on the back of his shaking hand.

Aha! The tweezers. They were a remnant from his last relationship, where Garrett's lover had been obsessed with grooming and personal appearance. Though it was initially something Garrett had been drawn to, it grew to be an unhealthy trait over time. Months in, Garrett realized he had glommed-onto a vapid shell of a man and might as well have been dating one of the mannequins on the third floor of Macy's.

Garrett slid the tweezers into his ear, fishing around for the worm with the sharp point of the tool. His knees buckled at the pain, and he dropped onto the tiny swath of floor by the bathtub.

BUZZZZZZZ!

BUZZZZZZ-BUZZZZZ!

The noise was frantic, coming from the box by the door, making Garrett's stomach flex from the pain.

BUZZZZZZZZZZZZZZ!

BUZZZZ-BUZZ!

Mike.

He'd almost forgotten his friend even *existed* in all the chaos and violence of the evening. He stared at his trembling, cut-up hands for a moment. *Hands that had snuffed two lives from this world.* Hands that could land him in prison for the rest of his natural-born life....

He tossed the tweezers in the sink, stumbled into the entryway, and pushed the button to open the front door of the building. He heard the hurried *thump-thump-thump* of Mike's oafish feet stomping up the levels and opened the door before the painful knock could sound and drive him berserk.

As soon as Garrett came into view, Mike threw his hands up into the air. "What the fuck, man? Why the fuck did you just leave me at The Garden? You can't send a goddamned *text?*"

Garrett's face was as white as an eggshell. "Something… happened."

"What do you *mean* something happened?" Mike's booming voice carried through the hall, and the next door opened. Ms. Ligerski stuck her face through the crack. Her ferret-like eyes glared at them.

Garrett raised a trembling, cut-up hand to acknowledge her. "Hey."

"Keep it down! It's fuckin' almost *midnight.* Take your pansy-ass conversation with your boyfriend in your apartment."

"Oh, we're not — " Mike motioned between them.

Ligerski didn't care. She just glowered at them until the door closed behind Mike.

"*Jesus*, she's a dick." Mike shook his head.

Garrett clutched his ears. "Keep it down, please. The noise…" He didn't finish. He shot back into the bathroom and Mike followed him.

"What the fuck is *wrong* with you, man?" His voice was quieter now. "I was lookin' everywhere for you! I went all around the concourse, askin' everybody about you. It was like trying to find a needle in a haystack. You weren't answering your phone. I figured I'd come back here to check on you. Thank *God* you're here, dude. I was freaking out!"

"Something happened. I don't want to talk about it. My head... The *sound*, Mike… The *sound* is doing something to my head. And I can't hardly stand right now. The world feels like it's spinning. I'm on a kayak in a hurricane, getting tossed around, even when I'm just standing still."

"Sounds like vertigo. They got meds fa' that at the pharmacy, over the counter. I had that a couple of times. You might have water in your ear or something. "

"Or *blood*."

Mike's eyes enlarged and his head cocked sideways. "What?"

"I threw up in the bathroom at The Garden, Mike. There were fucking *worms* in it! There were *worms* in my fuckin' puke! I freaked out. I left."

"Jesus, *worms?*" Mike itched the stubble on the side of his shorn scalp. "We gotta get you to a doctor, man. Or like a fucking *vet*. They got all kinda fuckin' de-wormers and shit for livestock these days. If you're pukin' up worms, there's gotta be some sorta anti-parasitic shit for that."

Garrett didn't respond. He stumbled back to the bathroom to retrieve the tweezers and tried to find the best light and angle to get back into his ear. He could still feel something in it.

Something *moving*.

"I'm just glad you're okay. There's tons 'a cops everywhere, and they had the bathroom by us taped-off with caution tape. Something happened there. I was really worried that something happened to *you*."

Garrett stood there, wavering in front of the mirror. Dizzied and nauseous, the vertigo bearing down hard on him.

"I'm not okay, dude." Garrett huffed twice, and his face twisted. He cried, frustrated. Tears leaked from his face, pattering softly onto his white shirt.

"I'm gonna call 911."

"No, don't! I can't afford an ambulance ride."

"You need ta' go to the E.R.! This ain't normal. You can't function like this. You're *pukin' worms, dude!* I'm takin' you to the emergency clinic at least."

Mike reached out, and Garrett whipped away from him. But the force of his own jerk threw him off balance, and Garrett stumbled into the empty tub, landing with a *bang*.

Mike gasped and reached in to help him up. "Jesus, dude! You okay?"

But his words were like an arrow that pierced straight into Garrett's brain. He covered his throbbing ears and growled.

Mike tried to help him out of the tub, but he refused the assistance. Once on his feet, he staggered toward the front door and grabbed the baseball bat beside it.

"You can't live like this, Garrett. This ain't negotiable. You should have gone to the doctor right when that little fuck next door fucked with your ear. We're goin' now, even if I fucking have to pay for it myself."

His well-meaning bellows and pleas nearly crippled Garrett, bringing him almost to his knees in pain at the sound.

He had to make it stop.

He just had to make the noise *stop.*

He raised the baseball bat and swung it at Mike, connecting *hard* with his best friend's neck.

WHACK!

The impact flung him into the tub, crunching something in his spine with a resounding *crack*. He reached out, hands scrambling to find purchase on *anything*. He grabbed the shower curtain and yanked it down with him as he tumbled into the basin.

Mike screamed, low and loud.

Garrett's vision narrowed again. His head pulsed with rage at the racket.

Garrett whipped the instrument again, smashing the dense wood into Mike's knees. A look of absolute horror and confusion spread across his wide face. He didn't know why Garrett was suddenly attacking him. He didn't know what to do to make it stop. He put his hands up in defense, locking eyes with the crazed lunatic as Garrett raised the bat to strike again.

Mike groaned in pain, feeling the devastated bones in his neck unable to support his head. He thrashed his lower limbs from the bottom of the tub, feeling a mix of relief that he wasn't yet paralyzed from the waist down... and terror that Garrett was poised to swing again.

Garrett brought the bat down hard and fast on Mike's right leg, shattering his kneecap.

WHACK!

"Help! *Somebody fucking help me!*" Mike screamed.

WHACK!

Another hit. This time to Mike's ribcage. He felt the fragile matter beneath the wood crack.

Mike could feel a sharp shard of bone puncture his lung, and suddenly, he couldn't get air. He gasped like a fish out of water and coughed up blood.

Garrett raised the bat again, this time bringing it down on Mike's skull...

Silencing him forever with one final *WHACK!*

CHAPTER 18

December 30th

11:39 p.m.

"This city is fuckin' brutal." Han paced behind Tredo, staring down at the devastated corpse lying in a puddle of worms and vomit. A puddle of coagulated blood had formed around the final resting place of his ruined face. The victim's pants were down, soiled underwear on full display. The toilet bowl beside him was streaked with blood and littered with human waste and busted teeth.

The sight was horrendous, but the smell was ungodly.

Mel Tredo stood guard at the bathroom entrance. She scrutinized the concourse outside, swarmed with the great unwashed. Their collective scent of body odor, fried food, and marijuana mingled in the air like a Trout-brand air-freshener. Though she hated the smell, it was superior to the noxious stench inside the bathroom.

"There's so much about this that makes me wanna vomit that I don't know where to start," Han said, lost in his thoughts.

"Yeah, it's not usually this bad two days in a row." Tredo jabbed her finger toward the next bathroom as two oblivious red-eyed patrons approached. "*Occupado,* my *amigos.* Use the one downstairs. Or better yet, your local, friendly *home* toilet."

"This place has to have a million fingerprints. DNA out the wazoo. CSI is gonna be busy today."

Tredo was lost in her own thoughts, thinking aloud. "You know, this isn't a calculated attack. It's hurried. *Public.* Violent. Whoever this is has some *serious* anger issues. Wonder if it's related to the D.B. at the convenience store. The Pop Shop ain't far from here."

Han leaned forward to silently investigate the still worms drowned in the puddle of stomach bile.

She continued, "Could be a frenzy killer. Someone impulsive. It's too coincidental that two of the most brutal crime scenes I've like, *ever* seen, just so *happen* to be in our sector. If I was a bettin' gal, I'd say whoever did this isn't done."

"Nah, I don't think they're the same guy."

"—Or girl," she corrected.

"In a *men's* bathroom? With *this* kind of strength? C'mon. You can't be *that* naive."

"Just testin' ya, Guppy." Tredo winked at him again.

"Perp is definitely male. Intoxicated. I can tell from the hoppy smell of this vomit and the half-digested oxy in this stew. Maybe the vic disrespected the Jets or something… pissed him off. Who knows? Either way, someone beat the shit out of him when he was at his most *vulnerable*."

"Maybe you stop huffing that puke like it's incense and let the big dogs solve this one."

Han nodded and stood up.

"Just hope this one doesn't get ya down like the last one. In a city of well over a million, there's gonna be some psychos. We just got to see the fallout back-to-back, is all."

"Right," Luca mumbled, never taking his eyes off the body. "This is just… *fury*. Who is *this* angry?"

Mel waved another stoned patron away. "You see the yellow crime scene tape? It ain't there for decoration. Move it along, Cheech."

Han chuckled as Mel snapped at the inebriated patron. "This guy is gonna have soaked shoes after stompin' someone like this. Blood on his clothes. We should have our guys downstairs funnel the people exiting and look for bloody shoes."

"Guy might be long gone already but yeah, guess it can't hurt." Mel grabbed the mouthpiece of her radio, eyes lingering on Han for a few milliseconds too long. Luca felt an electric current run the course of his body and looked away, chastising himself for being distracted by her beauty while standing over a savaged corpse.

CHAPTER 19

December 31st

1:08 a.m

The light on his phone blasted, flashing like a Halloween strobe. Garrett dropped the bloody tweezers in the sink. The stopper was engaged and tepid, pink water sat in the basin. Three small worms squirmed beneath the stilled surface, segments twisting and turning in unison like train cars rounding a sharp bend. Garrett glanced in the mirror at the remains of his best friend behind him, caved-in skull oozing a winding stream of crimson down the tub drain with the occasional gurgle emanating from beneath his demolished cranium.

Garrett's silenced phone flashed again. He flipped it face up and read the texts.

Jerome: I'm here. I'm horny. And I have wine.

Jerome: Hellooooo? Earth to Garrett.

Garrett's fingers tapped across the screen.

Garrett: Now is not a good time…

He hesitated to send it.

His eyes drifted to the word horny, and he felt his cock stiffen at the thought of Jerome's talented mouth wrapped around it. An almost uncontrollable surge of desire washed through him. He found himself there, staring at the phone, flooded by a dump of arousing chemicals in his body, telling him he needed nothing more in life at that moment than to fuck.

But then there was Mike…

Jerome: I can see u typing, you know

Jerome: R u blowin me off?

Jerome: Fuckin typical

Jerome: This wishy-washy shit is gettin real old

His fingers were typing again, almost as if they weren't his own.

Garrett: Come up. And bring that sassy, talented mouth with you. ;)

Before he realized what he was doing, his thumb pushed send. He dropped the phone on the counter with a look of shame and horror, nearly dropping it in the wormy water. He ran a hand through his disheveled, sweat-matted frock of prematurely-graying hair and unbuttoned the top button of his shirt. It was suddenly constricting him, choking him like two nefarious hands around his throat. He felt like he was going to hyperventilate, sucking in deep drags like he couldn't get enough air.

He surveyed the gruesome scene before him and limped awkwardly backed out of the doorway into the foyer. Pragmatic, as always, Garrett stared at the scene, devising a momentary disguise that might suffice. Jerome would stay for a bit, they'd fuck around, and as long as he could keep him away from the bathroom, he could decide how to deal with Mike's remains after that.

After coming up with a quick-but-clever coverup, Garrett made his way back in, carefully tip-toeing around the pooling blood near Mike's dangling feet.

His friend's mashed remains were slumped over the side of the tub, busted ribs skyward, head over the drain, legs akimbo, splayed in the world's most uncomfortable position of rest. He kicked Mike's feet in the tub, cranked on the shower, and closed the door. As he exited, his phone flashed again.

Jerome: r u gonna buzz me in or what? It's freezing out here!

Fuck!

Garrett: Yep. Sorry.

Garrett rushed toward the door too fast and fell to the floor, crashing down on his knees as another disorienting spell of vertigo overtook him. He scrambled to his feet, pulling himself up with the doorknob, and pressed the buzzer. He cupped a hand over his perforated ear-drum and groaned at the painful sound it made through the still-resonating tinnitus from the concert.

He scurried into the kitchen, holding tight to walls and counters. He rinsed his injured, bloodied hands in the sink. The sound of the rushing water from the faucet made his jaws flex and teeth grind. He dried his hands on a towel, suddenly awash with another wave of lust at the thought of Jerome satisfying his baser needs soon.

What the fuck is wrong with me? Mike is fucking dead in my shower right now, and my dick is hard.

He smacked himself in the head in pure revulsion and self-loathing, but it only made the vertigo worse.

A soft rap sounded at the door, and he was grateful for the late hour and need for social niceties such as that. He approached it, swinging it open to see Jerome bundled up in a fur-lined parka, teeth chattering.

"What the fuck? It's colder than a witch's tit in a brass bra outside, and you had me—"

Garrett was on him without another word, lips locked tightly with Jerome's, tongues entwining. Partly to stop the noise seeping from his mouth and partly because Garrett felt rabid, with a libido in overdrive. He could fuck a too-flat *pillow* to completion for all he cared. The need to fuck was uncontrollable.

Jerome switched gears too, no longer needing to finish the complaint. He pushed Garrett inside with nothing but the frenzied sound of the breath blowing hurriedly through noses, the soft patter of snow boots, and the running shower throughout the apartment. Behind Jerome's head, as if by pure muscle memory, Garrett locked the deadbolt, latches, and locks in the darkness, holding onto his boyfriend tightly, afraid that if he didn't, he would fall over.

The need to be inside of Jerome far overpowered the nausea he felt from the room spinning. He tore at the fabric of Jerome's layered clothes with animalistic aggression. Jerome's mouth broke free with a bright smile flashing like a strike of lightning in the sliver of moonlight seeping in from the window. "Woah, you haven't been this keen on me since the night we met at Razor's—"

Garrett put a finger on his lips to silence him, still dragging Jerome back toward the outstretched futon, clinging to him for stability. His mouth drifted to the soft, supple flesh of his neck, sucking and nibbling at the smooth, black skin beneath his lips and teeth in the way he knew always drove Jerome wild. He slid his finger between Jerome's lips slowly, and Jerome sucked on it, eyes shut, making Garrett want to collapse to the floor from the foreplay.

Jerome fumbled with the buttons of Garrett's dress shirt. "Who wearth a button-dow to a conthert?" he asked with the index finger still resting on his talented tongue.

"I do," Garrett said with a dominant, alpha edge to his voice. Something that took Jerome completely off-guard in a pleasant way.

"Mmmmm, you know," he took the finger deep and then slid it to the edge of his tongue again, "I like it when 'ou both me around like that."

"Yeah, I know."

"What did 'ou do to your hand?"

"Shut up," Garrett mumbled, halting the concerned line of questioning in its tracks. He replaced his finger with his tongue and kissed him deeply. He pulled away, and with no trace of a smile, he said, "Get undressed. *Now.*"

"Oooooh," Jerome grinned flirtatiously at the order and glanced at the bathroom door. He motioned to it. "Mike's gonna come out and see us though."

"Don't worry about him. He takes long showers. He just went in right before you got here," He lied.

It was quite the opposite, ironically. Mike was always the lowest-maintenance guy he'd ever known.

"But what if he sees? I don't need him trying to *mount* me or something. Or fuckin' scar him for life…"

"I said *shut up*. He's a big boy. He'll be fine."

"Normally, you're weird about being seen out in *public* with me, and now, suddenly, you're okay with your best friend possibly seeing us getting it on?"

"Hey," he rasped, "take off your clothes and get on your fucking knees on this futon. I want that ass." He slapped Jerome's left butt cheek hard, stinging the skin through the fabric of his tight jeans.

Jerome moaned, pleasantly surprised by this sudden change in his boyfriend's demeanor.

Garrett dropped to the futon and unzipped his pants. Jerome twirled around, taking his parka off and tossing it onto a duffel bag. He stared at it momentarily, uneasy about the prospect of Garrett's friend walking in on them. *That would be a hell of an introduction.*

Impatient, Garrett grabbed him by the jeans and unzipped his fly, reaching in to pull out the throbbing, thick hunk of meat hidden beneath. He slid his lips around it, taking Jerome deep in his mouth until he felt him pressed against the back of his throat. Jerome moaned again, and Garrett pulled his mouth away, still massaging the hard eight-inches in his stinging palm.

He stared up at Jerome with steely eyes. "Be quiet. You don't want Mike to hear, now, *do you?*"

"You just said he's a big boy—"

"Shhhhhhhh." Garrett's expression was gravely serious. Even the noise those whispered words made was like swabbing his ear with razors. "*No sound.*"

He slid his mouth back down the length of Jerome's shaft, and Jerome laid his head back, rifling his dark hands through Garrett's silvery locks.

But the taste of Jerome was not enough. He wanted to be *inside of him*, grinding against his espresso-colored skin like two animals in heat.

The sound of trickling water caught Jerome's attention despite the feel of the warm mouth deep-throating him. He craned his neck around, trying to locate the source of the noise through half-closed eyelids. The apartment was dark, but he could see water glistening as it rushed beneath the bathroom door, flooding into the foyer. He stepped back, pulling himself from Garrett's mouth like a sucker ripped away from a child.

Garrett stared up at him in confusion, watching Jerome tuck his hard-on back in his unzipped pants.

"Garrett, you're flooding." There was panic in his voice. He walked toward the bathroom, and Garrett lunged off the futon. The dizzying effects of the vertigo won the battle, and Garrett splayed across the floor, yelling, "Don't!"

It was all he could manage to get out before Jerome opened the bathroom door. A torrent of water oozed out, lapping down the sloping floor against his carelessly-discarded fur-lined snow boots.

"*Don't!*" Garrett shouted again, trying to clamor to his feet, using the wobbly table to steady himself. He felt like he was a piece of Styrofoam on white-capping seas, being tossed back and forth by the blood trapped in his cochlea.

But Jerome didn't hear anything beyond the low groan of the shower nozzle and the splash of his bare feet through the flooded mess. His eyes tracked from the pink sink *and the worms inside it* to the blood on the floor and flecks of red splattered across the shower tiles. His eyes finally settled at the horrific image in the tub.

Mike's broken body was lumped and bruised, lying in the spray. The half of his head that remained stared up through the overflowing water, wide-eyed and unblinking. Brain matter and slime dribbled out in rivulets through the open cave-mouth made in his head. The submerged stew was heaped in a mound, clogging the drain hole, sucked down by the pipe's vacuum.

Jerome shrieked loud enough for half the building to hear. Garrett lunged again, hurtling himself across the small space of the foyer, one that now felt vast with his disorienting disability. He latched onto Jerome, covering his mouth with a hand. Jerome tried to rip away.

The words came out muffled. *"VVVVVTTT the VVVUCK?! VVVVTTT the VVVVUCK?!"*

"Shhhhh. Shhhhhh. Don't yell." Garrett held on so hard that Jerome couldn't get air. He felt suffocated, both by the hand and from the sight before him.

At that moment, Jerome realized Garrett knew about Mike's body. He sunk his teeth into the meat of Garrett's hand, nearly severing the skin cleanly with the massive force.

Garrett dropped to his knees, face grimacing, mouth in a silent howl. A hunk of his palm flapped backward, hanging on by a thin patch of still-attached skin.

Jerome thrust himself away, ripping free from Garrett's grasp. He doubled over, screaming and sucking in a lungful of air. He looked at Garrett, who was scrambling toward him again, slipping in the overflow, dizzied by vertigo, leaning on anything within grasp for support.

Instead of latching onto Jerome, he took a right into the adjoining kitchen, clattering through a drawer with his bleeding hand. The injury didn't hurt nearly as much as the sound of the tools scraping together.

His head swam at the thought of Garrett being capable of such a vicious and brutal act.

Sweet, meek Garrett.

Jerome lurched for the front door, sliding on the wet floor and catching himself with the handle. He didn't give a shit that his pants were brought down during the tussle. He didn't give a shit that his parka was somewhere on the floor. *He only cared about getting out.*

Jerome fidgeted with the locks on the door, flipping the deadbolts and unlocking the chain.

And then…

Garrett's forceful groan rose above the sounds of locks and raining water, followed by the wet, indescribable sound of metal slicing through flesh.

Jerome was in shock. His stunned eyes locked on the glossy coat of paint, interrupted by the shadowy blob where Garrett's body blocked the moonlight. Unable to breathe, he touched his neck with dark and trembling fingers. He felt the hilt of the steak knife, buried through the side of his throat, held by Garrett's gnarled hands.

He touched the other side, feeling the cold metal point piercing clean-through. No air from his sheared trachea could pass through the flat, silver blade and he was once again suffocating.

Only this time… it was in his own blood.

Garrett released the handle, and Jerome stumbled backward slowly, unable to remove the knife, unable to breathe. He scrambled back to the futon.

Garrett watched intently, hands clutching the kitchen's door frame like a rocking subway pole.

He knew he should feel horror and agony over what he'd just done… But, for whatever reason, he felt *nothing*.

Nothing but *curiosity*.

Nothing but *lust*.

Nothing but *relief* at the sudden silence.

He lumbered to the bathroom, padding through the standing water on the floor. He turned off the shower and cautiously pulled two towels down from a rack, still steadying himself on the sink. He tossed the terry cloth swaths onto the floor by the front door in hopes that the water wouldn't leak outside and alert that nosy bitch Ms. Ligerski next door.

Her squawking was the last thing he needed right now.

He made his way over to Jerome, who was now propped on his arms, leaning backward on the futon, bathed in dim traces of moonlight like one of Michelangelo's marble sculptures. Muscles flexed. Body taut. Mouth agape in horror. *Eyes crying silent tears...*

Garrett had never been so turned on in his life.

He unzipped his pants, yanked them clumsily off, and tossed them into the sopping puddle in the foyer. His dick was hard, sprung high at full attention through the fabric of his boxers. He climbed atop Jerome as life was fading from his betrayed eyes and yanked hard on the handle.

The knife slid out with a sucking sound that made him wince.

Wet gurgles escaped Jerome's lips as Garrett flipped the blade over, placed it just above his boyfriend's Adam's apple, and sawed deep into his throat with the serrated end.

CHAPTER 20

December 31st

9:59 p.m.

BAM-BAM-BAM.

Fists on wood.

Garrett's eyes fluttered open, and he lifted his head from the gory cavity where Jerome's heart used to sit. He rose from his lover's chest, from in between his cold, ebony embrace, and stretched. Relief caressed him with soothing hands as his vertigo had dissipated greatly after the hours of exhausted rest on his side.

He clicked on the bedside lamp, stunned by the darkness throughout the apartment. He looked at his watch, eyes bulging at the loss of so many hours.

Jesus! How fucking long have I been asleep?!

He thought about the pills he downed after being with Jerome and smirked at the hazy memories he'd had with the corpse long into the hours of the early morning when the sun had come up.

In the carnage where his head had been, a puddle of red worms now squirmed in the organic muck, wriggling into the crevices between stilled organs and taking up residence in cooled ventricles, some bedding down in the connective tissue between the spine and scapulas.

The sight no longer disgusted him.

Like the country song once said, his *give-a-damn was busted.*

He felt like a sociopath, or *hell*, looking down at the corpse he'd lovingly cuddled into the early hours of the following afternoon. Perhaps *psychopath* was a far more apt moniker.

BAM-BAM-BAM.

The banging sounded again. He knew from the hate seething from the knuckles that it was that fucking spinster, Ligerski, no doubt coming to complain again about something else.

Before the knuckles could pound again, he arose from the futon. The fabric was soaked brown and off-white spilled bodily fluids. He shuffled across the floor and looked down at his naked body, smeared with blood.

BAM-BAM-BAM.

"I know you're in there!" She squawked, voice like an ice-pick in his skull.

He pulled on his Trout hoodie, squeezed into Jerome's soaked, bloodied jeans, and leaned into the bathroom. His face was smeared in shades of garnet and brown, especially around his mouth where he'd fellated Jerome post-mortem before turning him over to do far worse.

He dipped his hands in the sink water, now the color of pink cotton candy. Lifeless worms sloshed in the basin. He splashed the liquid on his face and scrubbed it clean-ish with his sleeve. He leaned in, looking closely at a ringlet of dark hair near his short, well-maintained sideburns.

It was moving.

He plucked the segmented insect from his ear, but it had latched on tight with its small fangs. He pulled hard and pinched. It panicked, released, and fell into the sink full of water with the rest of its brethren.

Garrett cleared his throat and returned to the door, opening it with a smile. The height difference between them was comical. He loomed over her.

"Ligerski."

She looked up at him and sniffed the air, scowling. "You were being awful-fuckin-*loud* last night. I don't appreciate it! If it ain't the fat asshole upstairs bangin' 'round like he's in some amateur production of *STOMP*, it's *you* with all this shriekin' and squealin' in here." She looked down, voice louder. "Why is the fuckin' floor soaked?!"

As soon as her eyes locked with his, a suddent burst of rage overtook him. He was zero-to-one-hundred. He had no control over himself, no ability to pull any punches. He was stuck in overdrive, his will no longer his own. His baser instincts were hyperactive. His id had overtaken. The imaginary devil on his shoulder only laughed now, seeking destruction.

Garrett was let loose on her, like a vicious Doberman with a broken chain. He grabbed her by the throat, walking her old body backward toward her apartment, choking the life out of her frail form. He pressed her back through the open doorway and shut the door behind them.

He shoved her forward with a force so hard she tripped over a heap of clutter piled around her old, wooden coffee table and launched onto the floor. She screamed, splayed there on the filthy linoleum, varicose-veined legs on full display beneath her hideous too-short nightdress. She clutched her upper thigh and howled in pain, yowling something about her hip. She was positive it shattered on impact.

Garrett tried to cover his sensitive ears with both hands and looked down at the infected bite wound in his palm. The almost-perfect imprint of Jerome's teeth made up the marred oval of flapped flesh. He used his wrist instead, feeling the roil of insects beneath the thin skin. He looked around, eyes studying her roaming parrot standing on his own wide-open cage roof, watching his owner being handled gruffly.

The bird stared at him.

"*Shut-up! Shut-up,*" the African-Gray cawed.

Garrett covered his ears to muffle Ligerski's wails and the screech of the bird. He raced forward and stomped her pelvis hard with his foot. Her arms went from one injury to the other as her screams grew louder.

"Leave me be! Someone call 9-1-1!" she cried, voice cracking from the warbling.

THUD-THUD. THUD-THUD. THUD-THUD.

Ligerski hadn't been kidding about the ruckus above her. The bass-y sound of muffled music seeped through the ceiling from the apartment above. The floor creaked and groaned loudly with the weight of whoever inhabited the place.

Garrett walked the room, bloodshot eyes studying decades of hoarded wares. Records, VHS tapes, doilies with porcelain dolls, each with dead-eyed stares. A fish tank obscured by green algae overgrowth had a red betta darting around inside, no doubt hoping for an end to its supremely boring existence. A crystal ashtray filled to the brim with pale yellow butts and tobacco ash sat on a bookshelf. He grabbed it with his good hand, dumped it in the aquarium, patted the bottom, and kneeled over the old woman.

She squirmed and thrashed, begging for her life.

All he wanted was to make the noise stop.

He just wanted quiet.

He bashed her face in with the beveled tray over and over and over again until the screaming halted. Her wrinkled extremities were still as a mannequin.

He glowered at the bird and rasped, "You still got somethin' to fuckin' say?!"

The bird sat in silence, bobbing its head up and down but saying nothing.

"What… the… *fuck?*" A man's voice called from the entrance. "Garrett? What the fuck?!"

Garrett whipped his head around, climbing off the old broad and tossing the ashtray onto the floor.

It was *Hunter Favreau*, the bite-sized fuck-stick's father.

Garrett stomped toward him and snatched Hunter by the lapels of his suit. Stunned, Hunter dropped his briefcase and tried with both hands to get Garrett off of him. Before he could, Garrett whipped him sideways down the curving staircase. Hunter's ankle bent in a strange direction as it tried to find purchase on the steps, and he careened head-first into the wall with a loud *CRACK!*

His body slumped lifelessly to the landing, rumpled like a dropped marionette, limb-over-limb, head cranked unnaturally backward.

Garrett stormed toward Hunter's apartment. The red halo around everything had returned. He had pulsing tunnel-vision. He rammed a shoulder full-force into the door and bounced backward. He took a few steps back, hunched lower, and without a thought about what devastation it could do to his body, he tackled the door like a football player, giving it his all. His shoulder smashed into the unforgiving wood near the handle and the door flung open, splintered and cracked, leaving a hunk of wood clattering to the floor from the jamb.

His shoulder felt like it might have shattered, but bone and muscular pain was the last thing on his mind. He felt rage. His hatred burned bright. He wanted to kill. He wanted to fuck. He wanted to rip his swollen head open and end it all.

End the *squirming*.

End the *pounding*.

End the *vicious instincts*.

End this miserable excuse for a *life*…

Hamilton was staring up in fear from his seat on the couch in front of another toxic news report, balls in hand, mid-scratch. A look of shock was frozen across his face as he tried to process the scene.

"Garr—"

He didn't even get the full name out of his mouth before Garrett snatched him from the couch and dragged him to the nearby window.

The one overlooking the quaint row of brick apartments punctuated by leafless, snow-dusted trees and skyscrapers glittering above, slicing through the black night sky.

Of course he got the *good* view…

"What the—" Hamilton struggled. "Let me go!"

Garrett's infected hand pulled the window up. As it maxed its height, Garrett slapped the boy hard across his chubby face.

"You fuck!" Garrett growled and thrust the child with all his might into the icy air.

Before Hamilton could react, he was sailing out the window, flailing his limbs wildly through the three-story drop onto the slush-covered concrete below. His body collapsed upon impact, upended. His neck cracked so loud that Garrett could hear it from above.

The kid lay unmoving on the squares of pavement, reminding Garrett of the rat he'd discarded out of his window just days before.

Out with the trash.

Good-fucking-riddance.

CHAPTER 21

December 31ˢᵗ
10:26 p.m.

Two teenage boys, dusted in moonlight, sat perched atop the frozen monkey bars of an elementary school playground, passing a joint. They each sucked weak puffs, erupting into giggling fits.

"Pass, Josh! Stop hoggin' it," the first said, his breath fogging the area between them like smoke from a dragon's nostrils. "Pass it back!"

"Shut up. It's fuckin' *mine*, dude." Josh argued before he sucked in a deep lungful of marijuana smoke and coughed violently for a few seconds, ending the fit with a gag.

"You gonna throw up, pussy?"

"Fuck off," Josh wheezed.

Behind them, Tredo and Han parked their vehicle along the sidewalk behind a blast of light from the tangerine-hued sodium-vapor streetlights. They quietly closed their doors. Tredo placed a finger against her lips. Han nodded. They both approached stealthily in the playground's eerie shadows.

"Yo, where did this shit come from? It's fuckin' *strong*."

"My brother, dude." The smoke held in his lungs changed Josh's voice. "He works at a dispensary. He gets good shit."

Once they were a few yards behind the boys, Tredo spoke, voice deep and authoritative. "We're gonna need your brother's name and address."

"It's legal, asswad," Josh hollered across the playground.

"Not this close to a school," Han fired back, "and sure as hell not for teenagers."

The boys looked at each other with a look of surprise. Exhaling smoke, both boys scrambled, leaping from their perch.

"Shit!" Josh shouted, followed by a weak cough, landing on his hands and dropping the lit joint in the gravel.

The boys sprinted away like a couple of wild dogs. Mel laughed, walking over to stomp out the joint.

"I suppose we're just gonna let them go, too, Officer Congeniality?" Luca already knew the answer.

"They're *kids*, Han."

"Pablo *Escobar* was a kid once, too."

"Jesus, you are such a goody-two-shoes, you know that?" Tredo deposited the remains of the joint into a nearby trash can. "You gotta be a *blast* at parties." She shoulder-checked him playfully as she walked by.

Han smiled, enjoying the fragrant waft of her fruity shampoo. "I am *very* fun at parties, thanks. Get a few beers in me, and I'm an absolute animal."

"Oh, I'll *bet*. You've got *drunken dancer* written all over you." Mel teased, raising one arm straight and the other bent, hand resting against her head. "You do the sprinkler, don't ya? Or the lawnmower. No, I'll bet you're more of a disco guy." She shot her arms out in the *Saturday Night Fever* pose.

"Next, you'll guess that I like to do the *hustle*. Or, hell, maybe even the *Charleston*. How *old* do you think I am?" Luca shoved his hands in his pockets. Even through his black gloves, the cold was biting.

"You tell *me*."

"Not old enough to freakin' *disco*, I'll tell ya that much."

"Nice dodge. Hey, when was the last time you played on a playground, Grandpa?" She leaned against the jungle gym bars.

"Well," Luca shoved around some gravel with his foot. "I'm not a child or a pedophile, so… not since I was a kid."

"Wanna hear something crazy? These things," she pointed at the bars, "have no age limit."

"No, but they have a *weight* limit," Luca teased.

"Fuck you. You calling me fat, Han?"

"No! God no." He blushed thinking about how perfect her figure actually *was*. "I just meant we're adults and therefore… larger… than… children."

Tredo giggled and hoisted herself up on the equipment. She launched herself down a cherry-red slide. Her utility belt scraped along the cold plastic. As she rose, stray hairs from her tight, blonde braid stood straight up with the static electricity.

"You look *insane*."

"You look like *you* couldn't spell *fun* if I spotted you the 'F' and the 'U.'"

Han opened his mouth to protest but was overwhelmed with the feeling that she was right. He hated to admit it, but since the day he entered the academy, he'd changed. He undeniably swapped his fun-loving attitude for his new rigid, palpably-uptight persona. The only time he felt relaxed anymore was after a rowdy bout of sex. Fortunately, those came more frequently these days. *Women really do love a man in uniform.*

Mel hung from the monkey bars, lifting her legs off the ground.

Han jumped up across from her. He snatched the bar midair and swung towards her. "This is kinda nice."

"It's called *joy*. You should try weaving some of it into your life."

Their bodies swayed like pendulums in childish unison.

"Can't wait until they watch back the body-cam footage of this." Mel laughed again. The moon bathed her in a hazy light that accentuated the china-smooth texture of her caramel skin.

Within moments, the playground darkened. The moonlight was blocked by clouds rolling in the overcast sky. A storm was coming.

Luca let go of the bars and plopped onto the pebbles. Unable to stop abruptly, Mel plowed into his chest with her knees. Han was launched backward, smacking into the ladder at the end of the bars.

"Jesus, Tredo!"

Tredo dropped to her knees, unable to stifle her laughter.

"You knocked me into metal steps! I whacked my fuckin' head! Why are you laughing?" But Luca couldn't help but chuckle himself after a moment. *Mel's laugh was infectious.*

"I'm sorry… it was just… your face was like, *oh shit.*"

Mel hunched down close to him, putting a hand on his thigh. "You okay?"

Despite the pain, Luca couldn't stop staring at her chocolate-brown eyes, made almost black by the dim illuminaton from the hazy streetlights.

Tredo's laughter abated, and suddenly, they realized they were both staring with Mel's hand still on his leg. The air between them felt alive.

The radio on their shoulders barked, jolting them back to reality in a harsh instant.

"Unit 16?"

Luca reached for his shoulder radio and pressed the button. "This is unit 16."

"16, we have a 10-55 at 341 West 49th."

"*Lame*," Han muttered as he rose to his feet.

"10-4…16 responding. *En route.*"

Mel sighed.

CHAPTER 22

December 31st

10:43 p.m.

The music thumped above, quaking the walls. Gloria Estefan's *Conga* oozed through the fibers of the building as Garrett stared up the next flight of stairs. He made a pit-stop in his apartment to get his shoes. With all the blood and water, the last thing he needed to do was slip and injure something else. His shoulder throbbed and his hands were devastated.

And that goddamned pain in his skull...

But still the rage within him carried him through. He was a man on a mission.

A quest for silence.

As he tied the laces, his destroyed palm pulsed, throbbing with his heartbeat. A missing hunk of meat and skin was the least of his problems, he thought, wanting to laugh at Jerome's splayed-open corpse, butterflied before him like a fetal pig in a science class.

The churning larvae populated the cavity behind his eyes, adding pressure as they claimed their space.

He headed back to the stairwell.

"Tiny insects in my head, tiny insects, buzzing-buzzing..." he whispered the words of the 90's Oingo song as he made his way up, tracking watery blood with every step.

There was only one apartment on the top floor, which struck Garrett as odd, having never risen above his own residential level. The rest of the space was dedicated to an office marked PRIVATE and a maintenance closet.

Garrett neared the door, eyes scrunched tight from the pain of the loud Latin beat emanating from within. He knocked, ready to chew his tongue off at the sheer intensity of the thumping and churning in his head.

As heavy footsteps made their way to the door, a fleeting thought flashed in his mind. He'd once read about a room in a tech company's building in Redmond, Washington, that was so quiet and soundproof that after a short time in it, you can hear the blood pumping through your veins. Though the maximum-insulated anechoic chamber was said to be *maddening*, the idea of such a blissful amount of silence seemed like a welcome dream to him.

The door swung open with a creak, and a rotund man in spandex stood before him, puffing large, exhausted bursts of breath into his face.

"Can I help ya?" His eyes seemed cautious, blinking hard to avoid the sting of sweat. Small weights were in his club-like fists and a sweat-drenched bandanna was wrapped around his slick forehead. The workout uniform hugged his curves tightly, nestling in every crevice of his body. Behind him, the music blared, and two women in full 80s-wear performed step-aerobics on a flatscreen TV.

Garrett barreled past the dripping man and bee-lined for the television.

"Hey! Get the fuck outta hea'! This is my house!" The man lumbered after him.

Garrett grabbed the plastic platform in the middle of the room, one that looked identical to the platform in the workout video. He whipped it forward, whizzing it through the air, smashing it into the TV.

"What the fuck are you *doin'*?! You're gonna fuckin' pay for that, you prick!"

The TV shattered, and the LEDs turned black instantly. A current of electricity popped in a bright, lemon-colored firework in the middle of the destroyed shards of plastic.

Garrett groaned like an animal, traumatized by the blaring sound of Estefan's too-chipper music. He spotted a vintage sound system and, without hesitation, swung the aerobics platform at it, too.

"*DO THAT CONG* —"

SMASH!

Silence. *Finally.*

The man looked at Garrett in stunned horror and hurled his hand-weights at him.

The first one missed.

The second hit Garrett square in the stomach. Even for a small weight, it packed the wallop of a donkey kick. He doubled over, coughing and gagging immediately. Disregarding the fact that something inside of him most certainly ruptured, he clutched his stomach and stomped toward his assailant.

He grabbed one of the weights off the ground just as the sweaty man lunged for his cell phone. He turned to race out the open door with it, frantically pressing buttons, but Garrett beaned him in the skull with the same hand-weight he'd been hit with.

The man went down hard, splaying across the wooden upper landing. Through sudden, devastated cries, he reached for the phone at the top of the stairs. Garrett went around him and stomped the phone with the heel of his shoe, smashing the thin glass into pieces with a sharp, excruciating burst of noise.

Garrett kicked the phone down the stairs and grabbed the man by his ankle, momentarily amused with his scrunched leg-warmers and neon tennis shoes. He dragged the man back into the apartment and retrieved the other weight.

"No, man, ple—"

Garrett brought it down upon the man's skull as many times as his exhausted muscles would allow, turning the man's face and brains into hamburger meat.

Huffing and puffing, Garrett kicked the door closed and laid on the floor beside the large, perspiration-covered body.

Suddenly, his eyes settled on the tiny island in the kitchen, loaded with fresh fruit and kale by the base of a brand-new-looking juicer. Beside it sat a knife, glinting in the moonlight.

Garrett smiled.

CHAPTER 23

"Hopefully, this isn't a call from you-know-who. Maybe we'll get lucky and she had a heart attack or a stroke."

"Jesus, that's cold." Luca shook his head and parallel-parked in a tight spot. "Although, that lady *is* wound up *tight*. She's just so *unpleasant*. Why couldn't we get a call about a box of abandoned kittens or a dispute at a strip club or something?"

"You ain't in Mystic, Han. You won't find a box of kitties around here unless they're being sold for bait or something. Plus, if you want to go to a titty bar so bad, why don't you just *go*?"

Luca laughed, "You know how much we make and how much the cost of living is here. I couldn't even make it *hail* at a strip club, much less *rain*."

"Make it *hail*?" Tredo asked, unfamiliar with the term.

"Yeah, where you throw *change* at the dancer instead of bills."

Mel laughed until she snorted. "You're seriously *pathetic*."

Suddenly, they saw a large crowd forming in front of the building.

Stepping out of their vehicle, Han shouted sternly. "Back up, people. Outta the way."

As the crowd grumbled and dispersed, Han and Tredo saw what the gawking people were gathered around.

A portly child was flat on the sidewalk, eyes wide open. There was an expression of shock frozen across his features. His broken limbs jutted out in wrong directions. His femur had busted through the flesh of his leg and pushed the fabric of his pants up like a bloody tent. His wrists were broken, bent backward against his forearms. A river of blood had woven its way down the sidewalk, dribbling into a nearby steaming gutter.

The first police to arrive on the scene were attempting CPR.

"1…2…3…4," the first cop said breathlessly, pressing in on the center of his chest with a steady rhythm and clasped hands. He nodded to his partner, stationed at the boy's head. She leaned forward, and squeezed the bulb on the CPR mask, watching the boy's chest rise and fall with the force.

With no signs of life, they repeated the process.

"What happened, Kutcher?" Tredo asked the uniformed officer by the boy's head.

"Dunno. Got a call about a kid down. We dunno if he jumped or he was thrown. We haven't had the time to find out whose kid this is. You guys should head inside and canvas the building. We're set out here until the EMT's arrive."

Tredo and Han nodded and jogged inside through the familiar entryway. White walls of peeling paint, streaked with oily hand prints, flanked them as they ascended the staircase.

"Super lives up on three. He'll probably know whose kid this is. By the look of it, kid had to come from one of the upper floors."

Once they passed the second floor, Hunter Favereau's limp body came into view.

"Jesus Christ," Mel said, mouth open in shock as she neared the body. Han followed behind, speechless for a few beats, before pushing through the stunned fog.

Han examined the body, careful not to disturb any evidence. "Think he fell? Or was *he pushed*?"

Mel Tredo drew her gun, arms extended toward the floor, finger resting along the barrel. She nodded her head up to the bloody hole in the wall about six feet above the body. "That answer your question? You fall, you hit low. *This…*"

She trailed off, eyes darting around the upper part of the staircase. She stepped carefully over the body. "Oh… my… God."

Han tugged his gun from his holster, aiming at the floor, too, and rose to his feet. "What?"

"Han, we got a *situation* here." Mel pushed the button on her walkie-talkie again, "Dispatch, this is Unit 16. We need a meat-wagon to 341 West 49th, apartment 3C. We believe we got a 10-54Q in front of the building, another 10-55 in the second-floor stairwell, and a D.B. in apartment 2B." She released the button, feeling queasy at the sight of Jerome's flayed corpse. She pressed it again. "Perp possibly still on premises. Send additional backup."

"Unit 16, ambulances en route. Expect delays in your area. Provide aid if necessary."

Mel scoffed at the notion. These people were *dead-as-a-doornail*.

Before Han even reached the top of the stairs, he was filled with dread. Tredo's colorless hue and look of shock said the sight before her was traumatic. He prepared himself for the sleepless nights ahead and stepped up the last few steps to the landing. "Clear inside. I'll watch your six."

From the landing, Luca's eyes could see the glistening form of the adult on the futon, bathed in lamplight. He darted to the stairwell on the right, eyes bouncing in every direction.

Still in a daze at the gruesome sight, Mel stepped forward into Garrett's apartment, eyeing the devastated carcass of Jerome, already drawing flies. Her feet stuck to the tacky, blood-caked floor. As she looked down to examine them, her eyes halted on Mike's submerged remains in the placid waters of the tub. "Jesus, fucking—"

"What?"

"We got another one." Mel looked out at him through the front door of the apartment, white as a ghost. Over his shoulder, she could see Ligerski's door was ajar. She motioned to it. "Check 3C."

Han nodded, grateful to distance himself from the corpses near Mel, but that feeling was stripped as soon as he glanced inside the old coot's dwelling.

"Tredo, another D.B. in here," Han rasped, nausea apparent in his voice. "Ligerski's DOA."

Ms. Ligerski's face was dotted with peck marks. Her red-stained locks were matted with ichor. The parrot sat on her shoulder, jabbing its hard beak at a hole in the side of her head that once was an ear. It licked at the sides of its stained beak with its odd, white tongue and greedily choked down a hunk of thin, Caucasian flesh. The old woman's body lay broken beneath his prehistoric clutches, face smashed beyond recognition by the crystal disc beside it, freckled with cavities dug-out by the parrot.

Behind her, an open window with a view of the city, alive with jovial chaos, let in the frigid winter breeze and sounds of the bustling metropolitan celebration. Clutching his 9-millimeter with a white knuckle grip,

Luca moved from one room to the next, clearing each methodically, taking special care with closets and beneath Ligerski's bed.

"This is the police!" Tredo shouted in the stairwell, backing out of Garrett's apartment. "Make yourself known!"

"*Clear.*"

They reconvened in the living area near Ligerski's corpse. Han fought the urge to vomit looking at her desecrated remains, but the state of the wrinkled woman was too much. He lunged to the open window above the fire escape and barfed onto the grated landing. Puke spewed through the wide holes, raining bile and half-digested gobs of dinner onto the ground level below. He breathed deep, sucking in large lungfuls of frozen air.

Drip.

Drip.

Something wet tickled the back of his head. He reached back to wipe it away. His fingers came back slick with wine-colored liquid. He twisted around, craning his neck up to see the source of it.

Drip.

Another droplet landed right in his eye. Despite his slightly obscured vision, he saw something he wished he hadn't through the red murk: A long, twisted rope, pink and wet, dripping blood, hanging out of the window on the floor just above like Rapunzel's braid.

"What… the…. Fuck?" Han yanked his head back in.

"You alright?" The words had barely come out of Mel's mouth before she realized he wasn't. *Not at all.* All color had drained from his Korean features, and sanguine liquid ran down his cheek like red mascara.

"Up… Upstairs." It was all he could mutter.

Mel bolted out of Ligerski's apartment. She looked at the bloody shoe prints on the stairs.

Han snapped out of his daze and followed behind, tucking tight to the wall, smearing foreign blood from his face frantically with his sleeve. He carefully put his feet in Tredo's footprints as he followed her up the stairs.

Toward the top of the steps, Tredo glanced down at the shattered remnants of a smartphone, smashed to bits, and yelled, "This is the police! Make yourselves known!"

The door was ajar too, and Mel nudged it open with the sole of her shoe. Inside, a large corpse was sprawled across the floor near the window. His morbidly obese belly was sliced open from groin to sternum, and his intestines spewed from his fatty folds, tossed outside of the window like tied-together bed sheets.

Han darted into the kitchen, away from the body, afraid he would throw up again and contaminate the scene. He turned on the sink and splashed water on his face and eyes, washing the blood away and quelling the urge to upchuck.

He shut off the sink and walked the kitchen perimeter, dodging protein bar wrappers and spattered health shakes as Mel swept the rest of the apartment, looking for the perpetrator.

The man's fridge and cabinet doors were all wide open. The contents of each were tossed across his kitchen, alive with worms eating and burrowing their squirmy bodies throughout it all.

"Dispatch, this is Unit 16. We have one D.B. on the front sidewalk, four on level three, and one on level four. Suspect still at large."

"10-4, Unit 16," the staticky voice replied.

Tredo carefully made her way down the hallway to the bathroom at the end. As she approached, it swung open.

"Freez — " Tredo shouted, adrenaline rushing, but didn't have time to finish the word before she was bowled over and punched in the face with brute force, shaking the gun loose from her hand.

Suddenly, they were both on the ground, scrambling for it.

"*Han!*"

"Freeze, or I'll shoot!" Han screamed from the living room, aiming at Garrett. Garrett got to Mel's gun first and pointed it at her head. She stared at him, trembling in fear. His eyes were wild. His face was stippled with gore.

"Something is *wrong* with me." Garrett's crazed eyes welled with tears. He wrapped the crook of his arm around Mel's throat and squeezed, pressing the barrel of her own service weapon to her head. She tore at his arm, slapping and twisting wildly, trying to recall all the self-defense strategies they taught her in the academy at the height of her panic.

"Let her go!" Luca screamed. "Tredo, I can't get a clean shot!" Han's thumping heartbeat made the sight of his pistol bounce.

Mel wriggled, tearing herself away from Garrett's grasp enough to expose one of his shoulders.

Han swallowed hard, exhaled, and pulled the trigger.

BANG!

Garrett screamed at the deafening sound of the weapon in such small quarters, ears ringing loudly with tinnitus, bringing with it the thick fog of red that clouded his vision.

Tredo stomped his foot, and Garrett growled in pain, still unwilling to release his grasp. She stomped again, then attacked a pressure point in his hand.

"Let her go!" Han screeched.

Garrett's eyes pinched shut from the searing pain in his head. His brain felt as though it were about to split in two.

"Everything is so *fucking* loud." He looked at Han, tears cutting clean streams down the dried, red flecks on his face. "There's something *wrong* with me!"

The understatement of the century, Tredo thought.

"We can get you help," Luca said, attempting to diffuse the man's anger with a calmer tone. He stared down his sight at the bloodied man before him. "Just let her go, okay? We will get you some help, some *real* help. I promise. Hurting anyone else isn't gonna get you that. Okay?"

Garrett's shoulders sank. He was exhausted, ready to submit to defeat.

Sharp static came across Han and Tredo's shoulder radios, nearly in unison. "Unit 16?"

Garrett's shoulders rose again, tensing in pain at the echoing screech. *"Turn it off,"* he whimpered.

"Unit 16, come in," the dispatcher said again.

"TURN IT THE FUCK OFF!" screamed Garrett. "Make it *stop*!"

Garrett launched Tredo forward at Han and ran toward the window. Tredo crashed into her partner, gasping and coughing as breath returned to her.

Garrett jumped outside on the fire escape, racing down the metal flights. He barreled down the last two flights with Tredo and Han hot on his trail.

Tredo slipped on the vomit and nearly fell over the rusted metal railing. "*Jesus!*"

"Tredo! You okay?" Han asked.

"Yeah," Tredo raced down another set of stairs, this time slower and more cautious, yelling, "You just *had* to fucking puke on the fire escape, didn't you?"

They two followed behind, watching Garrett stick his landing on the snow-dusted grass below with a *crunch* and take off like a loosed-arrow down the street.

CHAPTER 24

December 31st
11:39 p.m.

Han and Tredo gave chase, following Garrett in a flurry of activity down the neat rows of restaurants, whizzing past all of the eye-catching billboards sporting the flashy musicals on Broadway. Garrett weaved through throngs of pedestrians, dodging yellow cabs in the street like a frog in an Atari game.

Tredo wheezed, traumatized lungs full of frosty air. Han buried his frozen face in the turtleneck beneath his uniform. The mass of people clotted the streets the closer they got to Times Square. Television platforms and roped-off sections of the crowd punctuated areas of the massive spectacle on New Year's Eve.

Bright billboards and moving banners framed the X-shaped convergence where the major thoroughfares joined, flooded wall-to-wall with people from all around the world to leave the year behind and start anew.

Neons cast their brilliant, colorful hues through the drizzling rain that had just begun to spatter over the massive gathering. The famous Times Square ball was perched at the top of its pole, ready for its scheduled descent.

Winding his way through hordes of glitzed-out spectators, each donning their shiniest clothing beneath open coats and scarves, Garrett shoved his way through the damp crowd, winding his way through like a worm in packed soil, hands clasped over his ears.

Without realizing it, the crowd made way for him, none paying any real attention as he forced through like a bulldozer.

As he tried to push past one muscular man, the beefy New Yorker wouldn't budge. Garrett felt like he was slamming himself against a brick wall. The mammoth man turned toward him, looming like a meaty henge. "Quit pushin', dumb fuck! There's nowhere to *go*."

"Baby, baby, the ball's about to drop. Just let it go," pleaded the slender brunette beside him. She buried herself deeper in her winter coat like a freezing turtle and patted a gloved hand on his shoulder.

"Asshole ain't even listenin'. He's got his fuckin' hands over his ears," the man growled.

Garrett peered up at his ridiculous, flashing 2025 glasses with a vacant look, desperate to mute the chorus of chattering people around him. He glanced back, seeing a churn in the crowd where the officers were forcing their way through the people in his direction. He tried again to push past the meathead.

"You hear what I just *said*," the man asked, turning around completely to face him.

Han and Tredo peered through a seemingly-endless sea of faces, suddenly attuned to one shout rising above the rest.

Bingo. They had spotted their madman's black hoodie.

"Move," shouted Tredo as she brashly shoved her spectators from her path. The closer they were to the street, the thicker the attendees were packed in.

"Dispatch. Unit 16 in pursuit," Han said into his walkie. "White male, 6-foot approximately 2-inches, slim build, wearing a black hoodie, headed into the crowd at Times Square."

Suddenly, the massive man yanked Garrett's hands forcefully from his ears. "Listen, asshole!"

The man's voice boomed. Garrett's vision muddied at the agonizing cacophony of punishing noises.

"I said… *there's nowhere to go,* fuck-stick! Now, get the fuck away, or I'll knock your fuckin' teeth out!"

Garrett had to make the noise stop. His eyes shot open, and he snatched the light-up 2025 glasses off the man's face, snapped off one of the earpieces, and pounded one straight into the behemoth's eye, spearing the fluid-filled ball instantly. He screamed and flailed, falling backward against the crowd of drunken people.

The brunette beside him shrieked at the top of her lungs. A gap in the crowd widened as people realized what was happening. Shrill screams erupted from all around, sending Garrett's mind into a new plane of devastating pain.

Garrett slammed his palm forward again, thrusting the cracked plastic spear deeper into the man's orbital socket. He attacked the man, wrapping his extremities around him and gnashing at his face.

Tredo and Han pushed people aside faster, scrambling to get to Garrett. Shoving backward to get away from the madman, the frenzied crowd became a more forceful barrier than before. With every step Tredo and Han took, the fearful crowd knocked them back a few more feet like a powerful ocean wave. They could only watch as the herd of terrified people shoved their bodies through whatever gaps they could find to get away.

Han pushed forward, weaseling through the crowd until he was out in the widening berth around the homicidal lunatic. Han leaped onto Garrett's back, locking an arm around his throat and pulling backward with enough force to damn-near snap Garrett's neck.

But Garrett came whipping back with a surprise.

He had the man's nasal cartilage and upper lip between his teeth. Blood dripped down from his full mouth. He spat the rubbery hunks into the crowd and growled, rabid with anger and adrenaline. Tredo caught up with Han, straddling Garrett's calves, wrenching his arms back forcefully, and locking a pair of industrial-strength zip ties around his wrist.

As the nose-less, lip-less man screamed in terror, echoed by the horrified crowd around him, Garrett yelled, *"Shut up! Shut up! Shuttttt upppppppp!"*

Winded, Tredo used her free hand to depress the button on her radio. "Dispatch… we have a… 10-54H. Caucasian male… down… Times Square. We need another ambulance. He attacked a bystander."

"TEN!" The crowd cheered.

"MAKE IT STOP!" Garrett screamed at the top of his lungs.

"NINE!"

"Make it stop! Please, God —"

"EIGHT!"

"P-please, God, make it stop!" Garrett sounded like he was turning himself inside out with his guttural pleas. Han looked at him mercifully as he led Garrett through the crowd in zip ties.

"SEVEN."

"Kill me!"

Han fished around in his pocket and pulled a folded twenty out of his wallet.

"SIX!"

"Just fucking kill me, PLEASE!"

Luca waved the bill at a nearby woman and pointed to her earmuffs.

"FIVE!"

The giant, lit-up disco ball was halfway down the pole.

"Your muffs!" Han shouted. She looked at him, confused, and slowly removed them.

"FOUR!"

Once they were off her head, he snatched them up, and she took the money, face almost snarling at him.

"THREE!"

"Shoot me! Fucking shoot me!"

Han used both hands to pry the furry muffs apart and stepped toward Garrett. Garrett flinched.

"TWO!"

Garrett finally realized what Han was trying to do and leaned forward, staring at him like his Korean savior.

"ONE! HAP-PY NEW YEARRRRR!" The crowd screamed.

As the earmuffs clamped down over the sides of Garrett's blood-spattered head, tears poured from his eyes.

Kazoos and blow toys sounded. Confetti bombs popped. Oblivious people cheered, screeched, and sang.

Han looked into Garrett's eyes with pity as the crowd broke into a messy, collective rendition of *Auld Lang Syne*.

CHAPTER 25

January 3rd
7:48 p.m.

The anti-parasitic medicine wasn't sitting well with Garrett. Neither were the handful of anti-psychotics and cocktail of other mysterious pills that claimed to keep all of his other mental and physical disorders in check. Garrett sat like a zombie on the top cot of the bunk bed in his cell, skin pallid. Drool seeped from the side of his mouth onto his orange jumpsuit.

He was a shell of the man he once was.

The scans of his brain looked like *Swiss cheese.* Like a dog's heart, all holes and burrowed cavities after its heartworms had been eradicated. Where there once used to be dreadfully formal pockets on his button-down shirt, there now sat the word REUBENS above a prisoner number that his brain-damaged mind couldn't recite, even if paid to.

A man approached, tall and muscular, with a look of hate burning in his deep-set eyes, ones almost level with Garrett's own.

"Get down," he growled.

Garrett didn't budge. He only sucked at the forming drool perched on his lips.

"C'mon man, leave him alone. Look at him. He's a fuckin' retard," another man mumbled quietly, a voice of reason in the darkened cell. His eyes shifted around, looking out for guards.

The man in the cot below, Manny Alvarez, pretended to be asleep. Fear quaked him beneath his thin sheets. He scrunched his eyes tight, pretending to breathe hard as if lightly snoring.

"I said get the fuck *down*, Reubens."

Garrett's lost eyes seemed focused on the inmate's garb. It read:

Ligerski, Ronald
#34962946532

Ronald jerked Garrett onto the floor by his clothes, and Garrett clattered to the concrete like a man in a coma, smashing in the bones behind his eyebrow upon raw impact.

Ron jerked him to his feet, and Garrett stayed silent. He neared Garrett's ear and, with tears in his eyes, managed, "You killed my fuckin' mutha, you piece'a shit."

Without another word, Ron smashed Garrett's face in with his meaty fist against the structural rail where the mattress of the top cot rested. He pounded unmercifully, and with the inside of Garrett's head turned to a wormy mush, the rail caved-in the back of his skull.

With every subsequent punch, wet, red meat flung onto Alvarez in the bottom bunk. He flinched in terror, eyes closed tightly. He could have *sworn* he felt the matter move against his skin.

SMASH!

A wet stew of brain and meat flung out, spattering against the wall in front of Manny as he continued his charade, pretending to be a heavy sleeper. Alvarez pried one eye open, staring in horror at the tiny worms writhing in the brains on the wall two inches in front of him.

At that moment, he realized the goo splattered on the side of his face *was* moving.

It was squirming against his cheek. His hair. His neck. Leaking into his ear…

Writhing.
Seeking…
A*live.*

"Ew, what the *fuck?*" Ron muttered, looking at the worms on his battered fist.

"*He's fuckin' dead! Let's go, Ron,*" the man in the doorway whispered.

The two intruders were gone as quickly as they'd arrived.

Alvarez shivered in horror, afraid to move. Afraid to let Ligerski know he'd witnessed anything. Afraid to see the gruesome mess they'd made of his cellmate.

And, more than anything, afraid that the worms all over the side of his face were making their way inside of him.

CHAPTER 26

January 15th

11:52 a.m.

"This week's three-day prison riot was the most brutal in New York history, experts say. Warden Darren Schumer says that after reviewing the security footage, an inmate by the name of *Manny Alvarez* appears to have been the ring-leader inciting the violence."

"*Jesus.*" Tredo shook her head.

"Insiders have given us a glimpse into the violence behind the scenes, stating that one guard was *decapitated* by the inmates, another eviscerated. Experts say these were a surprisingly *uncoordinated* attack, seemingly fueled by rage. Officials are currently speculating as to whether or not they will be able to locate *all* of the violent escapees—"

Han's hand wrenched the knob of the radio into the off position.

Tredo stared forward in silence from the driver's seat of the squad car.

Luca finally turned his head to Mel. After a moment of brutal quiet, he said, "Madmen on the loose in a city full of chaos and disorder. Another uplifting story from the news. You know what'll help?"

"Shit," Tredo stared forward, eyes locked on the jaywalking New Yorkers in front of her, "we already missed happy hour, Han."

Luca managed a bleak laugh through the grim fog of it all. "How about we settle for me finally buying you that fuckin' hotdog?"

Erica Summers is an independent filmmaker, artist, film industry grip, and writer with an unwavering passion for horror. Several of her award-winning feature films have screened worldwide including Obsidian, Mister White, & Loverboy (available on most streaming services.)

Though born and raised in Wyoming, Erica spent most of her life in the swampy American South. She now resides in Connecticut where she works in film and writes and illustrates genre fiction. In her downtime, the bizarre bisexual is typically slathered in garden dirt, kayak fishing, or devouring horror movies with her boyfriend and their two jack russell *terrors*.

Heather Wohl (Writing as H.M. Wohl) coordinates a growing oil field laboratory based in Casper, Wyoming. While her job is straightforward and clinical, she enjoys letting her mind wander into creative outlets. An avid storyteller since childhood, she has always enjoyed spinning fantastical tales.

She is a proud supporter of chronic illness support, mental health awareness, and pitbull advocacy, considering the latter to be her furry muses. Heart and soul are poured into every page of her work, and she looks forward to the opportunity to entertain you.

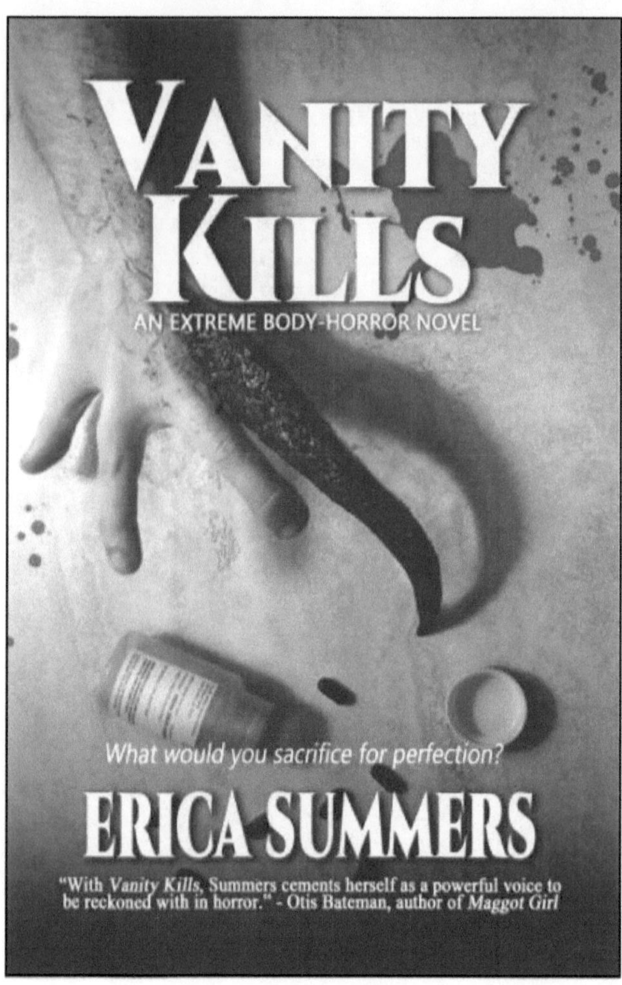

Vanity Kills
An Extreme Body-Horror Novel
By Erica Summers

Available worldwide in paperback, ebook, hardcover, and audiobook.

The Rictus Grin & Other Tales of Insanity
A Collection of Short Horror Stories
By Erica Summers

Available May 28, 2024 worldwide in
paperback, ebook, audiobook, and hardcover.

BAD GOD'S TOWER
A Western Horror Novelette
By Erica Summers

Available in paperback, hardcover, e-book, &
audiobook

From Ashes

Book One of the Illuminator Saga

A Dark High-Fantasy Series

By Heather Wohl

Available now in e-book, paperback,
hardcover, and audiobook

Desdemona in Embers
Book Two of the Illuminator Saga
By Heather Wohl

Available now in e-book, paperback, hardcover. Audiobook releasing in March 2024.

www.ingramcontent.com/pod-product-compliance
Lightning Source LLC
Chambersburg PA
CBHW022047050726
47591CB00002B/421